The Girl
Without a Name

GUNNEL BECKMAN

Translated from the Swedish by
Anne Parker

Illustrated by Borghild Rud

HARCOURT BRACE JOVANOVICH, INC.
NEW YORK

Originally published by Albert Bonniers Förlag in Sweden under the title of *Flickan utan namn*

FIRST AMERICAN EDITION
ISBN 0–15–230980–2
Library of Congress Catalog Card Number: 75–124840

PRINTED IN THE UNITED STATES OF AMERICA

The Girl
Without a Name

ONE

THE airplane buzzed upward like a huge, angry wasp over the summery blue waters of Öresund and then leveled off high above the southern tip of Sweden. It was now more like a kindly bus rumbling along quite calmly.

A thin little girl with black pigtails sitting by one of the small round windows of the plane drew a deep sigh of relief and opened her eyes, which had been tightly shut. Her eyes were large and dark and full of fear.

"That was our very last takeoff," a comforting voice whispered in the girl's ear. "We'll be arriving in Stockholm in about an hour."

The voice belonged to a fair-haired young woman in red who was sitting next to the girl, holding her hand very firmly.

"Now you can unfasten your safety belt and look out of the window, and you'll get your first glimpse of Sweden," said another voice from the outside seat.

It came from a tall, bearded man dressed in a gray suit. The girl called him "Bosse." "Do you remember the map of Scandinavia that we have looked at so many times?" he continued. "You know it looks rather like a bear. Well, we are just flying over the front paws of the bear now."

The girl slowly withdrew her hand, unfastened the safety belt, and leaned forward cautiously to look out of the window. She wasn't quite sure that her stomach had settled down after the takeoff. Then slowly a smile spread across her pale lips, and the tense, anxious line of her mouth relaxed.

"Oh . . ." she said, leaning forward even further.

The weather had been bad throughout the long journey, and for miles and miles they had rumbled through clouds—sometimes sunlit and white as snow or whipped cream on a cake, sometimes dark and heavy with rain, looking like the backs of an enormous flock of sheep—but always clouds. It was only when they landed at various airports that the ground had come rushing up toward them at a terrifying speed with its houses and gardens, church towers, and tiny cars.

But now all the clouds had disappeared. Far down beneath them lay a brightly colored toy landscape drenched in summer sunshine.

She rubbed her eyes again and again and flattened her nose against the glass. Fields, dark and light

8

patches, formed the pieces of an enormous puzzle . . . blue-black borders of pine forest . . . yellowy green groves of trees . . . glimpses of silver lakes and rivers.

"How *green* Sweden is," she said at last, "so very green, and no houses at all!"

"Oh, yes." Bosse smiled. "You'll find there are houses all right, but we're flying so high that we can't see them. Many of them are hidden by trees at this time of the year. Also, lots of them are painted red, and that doesn't show up very well at a distance."

"When we have arrived and unpacked and settled down at home, we'll read you a wonderful book about a boy who was turned into a tiny little creature—as small as this—and traveled all around Sweden on the wings of a large bird, a goose called Akka," Bosse's wife, whose name was Margareta, said to the girl. The girl usually called her Ma.

"But Akka didn't fly as high as a jet plane." Bosse laughed. "And not as fast either, so it was easier for the boy to have a good look around."

The girl said nothing. She just went on staring at the moving map with her sad black eyes.

Other forests and plains appeared and disappeared, different villages made of colored toy bricks, different flashes of water in the sunlight. Soon the blue spread out and became a sea with many little islands crowding like seal pups along the coastline.

Margareta and Bosse watched the girl's face and then looked at each other. They were both thinking the same thing:

How would it all work out? What was going on in her mind? What was she seeing? This rich, sunny landscape in green and blue . . . or was she remembering another landscape, a yellow and gray one . . . a countryside of mud and rocks, steppe and desert, with occasional patches of green? Was she perhaps feeling homesick?

"We are now approaching Stockholm!" A voice on the loudspeaker interrupted their thoughts, and the girl quickly drew back from the window and began to fumble with the safety belt.

The long journey over land and sea was nearly at an end, and for the last time she leaned back in her seat, gripped the armrest tightly with one hand and Margareta's hand with the other, and closed her eyes.

For the last time the ground came rushing up toward them. The map came to life and began to move. Cars drove along, and flags waved. Antlike people rushed about. But the girl kept her eyes shut.

Even if she had looked, she would probably not have noticed a large old red house with a white veranda covered in ivy, tucked away in a garden not very far from the airport. And even if she had seen that very house, she would probably not have been able to observe that a little girl was sitting on the steps.

It was a girl of about her own age, dressed in a checked summer skirt, wtih her fair hair tied in ponytails at each ear—a little girl who looked up at the airplane with eyes red from crying.

11

TWO

SARA was angry, unhappy, and disappointed. And to make matters worse, she had a guilty conscience.

She was sitting in the dark at the far end of a built-in closet that her father used to call "The House of Sorrows." She hated the whole world.

The tears had stopped. Now there was just the occasional deep hiccuping sigh. But she was just as furious, terribly unhappy, and awfully disappointed as before. Her guilty conscience was gnawing away at her stomach like a mouse.

And yet it was only a few hours earlier that Sara had awakened in bed full of sparkling happiness. Her whole body had tingled with pleasure and excitement as she watched the sunlight trickling like a waterfall through the Venetian blinds onto the tartan suitcase and the green bag, all packed and ready on the floor. The bright yellow life jacket and the blue flippers lay on the mat, and Ulrika, the old doll, sat on a chair in her traveling clothes, with brand-new velvet arms and new curly hair that had cost two kroner for half a yard.

How Sara had longed for this day! For a whole month, even before school closed for vacation, it had been settled that on Monday, the fourteenth of June, at eleven forty-five, Sara would get on the train at the Central Station and travel by herself all the way to Gothenburg. And she would have super sandwiches with her, white bread with salami sausage, and special cheeses, and a large bottle of lemonade and a straw to drink it with, and fruit and candy and chewing gum and a paper napkin and two new books.

And when she had eaten everything and the train had rushed past hundreds of stations and masses of lakes and farms and water towers and meadows and foals, she would arrive at Gothenburg late in the afternoon and find Aunt Cia waiting on the platform with a redheaded twin on either side of her, and Uncle Pelle would be waiting outside in his enormous old car full of supplies they had shopped for.

Together they would drive out to the sea, glinting silvery and mirrorlike in the sun. And it would smell good and fresh and quite different from their own old water at Väddö. Although that was the very best in the world, it wasn't as clear and blue and warm as the water on the West Coast.

What a wonderful time they were going to have

13

bathing and diving with the flippers and popping those little seaweed balloons and catching sweet little crabs with a piece of string from the landing stage! They would search for white, spiky shells among the rocks where dead jellyfish lay around in great yellowy red blobs, and they would climb the high, wild rocky hills where no trees or bushes grew.

Sara remembered exactly what everything was like, although it was two years since she had been there with her parents.

Nearly every night before she went to sleep, she had imagined what fun it would be to play with the twins again and sail in Uncle Pelle's little dinghy and catch mackerel, so shiny and smooth and delicious.

Slowly the tears began to run down Sara's cheeks again as she sat huddled in the corner of the closet, thinking about how she had planned and planned. She had no handkerchief, so she licked the salty tears that ran down to her mouth, and she blew her nose on the hem of her skirt. Of course it was the nice new checked skirt, bought specially for traveling in, but what did it matter now if it got messy and creased? *Nothing* mattered any more!

She had finished her breakfast that morning, although it was awfully difficult to have both yogurt and a boiled egg, but Mother said that you had to eat properly when you were going to travel. Dad was just making the sandwiches when the telephone rang. He put down the cheese cutter and went to answer.

It's strange that you can be so fantastically happy

14

one moment and so completely down the next—strange that things can happen so quickly.

"A telegram from Cia," he said, looking at Mother, who was standing there with a knife poised over a piece of salami. "The boys have measles."

"No!" Mother exclaimed, dropping the knife. "What an awful thing to happen! What rotten luck! Measles in the middle of the summer! Whoever heard of children getting measles in their summer holidays? And Sara hasn't had measles! Well, then she can't go! What a shame! Whatever shall we do now?"

It took a whole long minute before Sara realized what had happened.

If the ceiling had fallen in and buried her in plaster, she couldn't have been more dumbfounded. She sat quite still without saying a word while that sentence, "Well, then she can't go!" slowly sank into her brain.

"Then she can't go . . . then she can't go!" Not go??? *Not go???*

The next moment she had flung herself headlong on the kitchen floor, howling like a puppy. She lay on her stomach on the grubby old linoleum in her new skirt and clean blue sweater.

"I want to go. I want to go," she screamed. "Stupid, stupid, stupid!"

"But my dear child, calm down," Dad said in his kindest voice, and bent over to pick her up. But she struggled and kicked so that he had to let go.

"Darling, of course we understand that you are terribly upset about this," Mother said, trying to sound

calm and controlled, "but you'll see that . . . we can have a really good time at home, too. . . . This is almost like the country, and on Saturdays and Sundays we can go out somewhere in the car and take a picnic or perhaps go to the zoo at Skansen or the fair at Gröna Lund and . . ."

"I want to go to the *West Coast,*" Sara howled, and pushed one of the kitchen chairs so that it fell over with a crash. "I want to swim and play with the twins . . . and . . . and . . ." The last words were smothered in wild sobs.

Mother and Father looked at each other helplessly. What were they to do? Their beautiful plans for the summer had been shattered.

All through the spring they had been discussing how Sara, the little one of the family, could spend her summer. All the older children were off in their different

16

directions. Sven was doing his military service, Annika, who was studying to be an engineer, was working on a building site, and the high-school boy Jonas had gotten himself a job on a boat. As neither Mother nor Father could take their holidays until August, they had decided to let their summer cottage until then. So, of course, some pleasant holiday activity had to be found for Sara.

When Aunt Cia wrote and asked if Sara would like to spend six weeks with them at Tjörn, Sara was overjoyed. She was fond of Aunt Cia and Uncle Pelle and got on very well with the twins, Paul and Peter, although they were awfully boisterous and always talked both at once.

What fun it had been arranging everything for the trip!

She had been bought a green bag and a new beach robe, blue with a hood, and a flowery bathing suit with gathers all down the front—the first *real* bathing suit she had ever had. Then they had bought presents for the boys—a flashlight with different colored lenses to shine the light through and a large jigsaw puzzle for rainy days.

And Sara hadn't been at all scared of traveling alone the long way to Gothenburg—at least, only the tiniest little bit.

Sara had stopped banging and kicking, but she still lay on the floor with her face on her arms, sobbing a little. She could hear Mother and Dad talking and talking to comfort her.

But she didn't want to be comforted.

It really was so horribly unfair. Nobody in the whole world could be as unhappy as she was. She felt Mother's hand stroking her hair, but she tossed her head and pulled away—she didn't want to be stroked. *"Leave me alone!"*

"Sara!" Suddenly there was a different note in Dad's calm voice. "Now you must try and control yourself! It's a great pity that you can't go to Aunt Cia's. We all think so. But that doesn't mean that you can behave just as you please. You are nine years old now and a big girl, and you must realize that one does sometimes have disappointments like this. Now get up and wipe your tears, and we'll talk things over quietly and decide what to do. Here's a handkerchief."

However, Sara didn't want to talk things over quietly. As quick as lightning she shot up and out through the door of the kitchen, which she slammed after her with a loud bang. A moment later her footsteps could be heard running upstairs, and after that all was silent.

"Poor kid." Dad sighed, stroking his chin thoughtfully.

"I expect she is sitting in The House of Sorrows," Mother said. "We had better leave her until she has gotten over the worst disappointment. You know what it's like when you're disappointed as a child . . . and she was looking forward to it so very much!"

18

THREE

THE House of Sorrows, or The Corner of Sighs as it was also called sometimes, was really quite a cozy little place.

To start with, it had just been an ordinary built-in closet with a sloping ceiling, the kind you often find in old houses.

Sara's older brother Sven was the one who first discovered that the room was far too nice to be used for storing old boxes and rubber boots and broken lampshades. When he was small, he persuaded Mother to move those things up into the attic, and Dad helped him to paper the brown walls with some wallpaper left over from the nursery. What a difference that made! With a carpet on the floor and a ceiling light, the old closet was suddenly transformed into a nice little room. The only trouble was that it had no windows.

19

"But you'll suffocate in here, Sven," Mother said, and was rather worried as he settled into his private domain with the little doll's table, the box of building bricks, the blue stool, his teddy bear, and a cushion and his worn old cot blanket—"In case I get tired, you see," he said.

"But you must keep the door open; otherwise you'll use up all the air and feel sick," Mother persisted.

"Oh no, 'cause I want to be with peace and quiet," Sven had said firmly as he went in and shut the door behind him.

Mother thought for a moment. Then she went to the toolbox to get the fretsaw.

After a little while Sven had a window—in the door! And Sven, who had protested loudly to start with, discovered that his little room was even nicer now—especially after Mother had put up some bits of the kitchen curtain over the window.

As the closet door faced the window on the landing, Sven could sit on his blue stool and see the branches of the pine tree waving in the wind, and he could just glimpse the white feathers of the magpie in the apple tree.

But all this was long ago.

A lot had happened under the sloping ceiling since then—a lot of exciting secrets and many happy games. Many injustices had been thought about, and a lot of rage had cooled and died. . . . Many comics had been read and many pictures of film stars thumbed through. A lot of fruit juice had been drunk, and many tears had been shed.

It was only when little Sara settled in the room that it was given the name The House of Sorrows, for tears came very easily to Sara.

That wasn't really surprising when everyone else in the family was so much bigger and more sensible. All the time she had to try hard in order not to be left behind, and she couldn't let people regard her as a baby.

Mind you, quite honestly Sara often enjoyed being the little one of the family. The others were nearly always good to her, and when Sven occasionally came to meet her at school, she was overjoyed and proud. All the others in her class had little troublesome brothers and sisters who screamed at night and spoiled their belongings, but hers were grown up and took her to parties and things. And nobody has the heart to chase you off to bed if there is only *one* of you, so you see a lot of TV that the others don't. Sometimes, too, she was taken to the theater and saw plays that were not for children at all, as there was no one at home to look after her.

So there was a bright side all right. But just at this moment—this sad Monday morning of June 14—as Sara sat in The House of Sorrows feeling angry, unhappy, and disappointed, she couldn't see any bright sides at all. On the contrary, there could be nothing more ridiculous and stupid in the whole world, she thought, than to be the youngest child in a family of grownups!

If she hadn't been that, she would have had lots of brothers and sisters the same age as herself who didn't dash off abroad or something but stayed at home in the

21

country, and Mum and Dad would not have let the cottage but would have had to stay there with the children the whole summer and look after them and care for them.

Then this need never have happened—sad things like silly boys getting measles in the middle of the summer.

Sara never gave a thought to the sorry plight of Peter and Paul who had to go back to town and stay in bed with curtains drawn and have headaches and high temperatures and spots all over their bodies. No, they were horrid and stupid to spoil her summer holidays with their silly, silly measles!

Gradually Sara's anger began to sink down, her tears dried into sticky streaks on her cheeks, and her disappointment lost some of its sting.

She was beginning to become conscious of what was

happening in the house. There was a lot of running up and down the stairs. The telephone rang several times, and then the car started.

The curtains were drawn over the little window so nobody could see in, but in there it was quite easy to hear what was going on outside.

Sara's guilty conscience, which had been gnawing away inside her under all the unhappiness, began to come to the surface. She thought about how she had lain on the kitchen floor kicking and banging her fists like a three-year-old and knocked over a chair and pulled her head away when Mother had wanted to pat her, and how she had run away, although they had tried to comfort her.

Suddenly she felt so ashamed that she turned as red as a beet as she sat there alone in the dark.

She got up cautiously and limped across to the hole in the door. One of her legs had pins and needles, and her whole body felt stiff and strange. She leaned out and listened.

But now all was silent. The car had driven off.

A thought suddenly pierced her heart: "What if they've gone off and left me alone because I've been so naughty?"

But then she heard a door shut downstairs and footsteps on the stairs. Sara tiptoed back into the corner. She still didn't have the courage to face Mother and Father in daylight.

"Are you there, Sara?" It was Dad's voice, and he sounded so kind and gentle that the tears welled up in her eyes again and began running down her cheeks.

"Yes," she murmured huskily—her voice sounded as though she had a cushion over her face.

"Could I speak to you for a moment, darling?"

"Just . . . a minute . . . soon . . ."

Sara scrambled up from her corner again and walked unsteadily toward the door, wiping her new tears on the sleeve of her sweater as she went. Very, very slowly she pushed the door open.

The next moment she was in Dad's arms with her face buried in his coat. "For—give—me," she sobbed as fresh tears came welling up.

"There, there, little Sara, you mustn't cry any more now," Dad said, bringing out a large clean handkerchief from his breast pocket to wipe her face. "We understand that you were very upset, but now I'll tell you how Mother and I have decided to arrange things for you. She had to leave to go to work a little while ago, but I have arranged to work at home—not only today, but also the whole week. And in the meantime, we will try to make some plans for you for the next few weeks, and who knows, perhaps it will just be a very mild case of measles, so you might have time to visit Aunt Cia before our holiday after all."

"For . . . give . . . me for kicking and . . . screaming," Sara whispered again, and blew her nose with a loud trumpeting noise. It almost felt as though she were getting rid of a lot of trouble at the same time.

"You pop into the bathroom and wash your face with cold water," Dad said. "You look just like that

24

bear with all the wasp stings in your old picture book. And then you'll have to come downstairs and help me cook some lunch for us both."

With a relieved, sniffling giggle Sara disappeared into the bathroom.

Funny that you can feel so angry and miserable one moment and then the next moment, if not exactly happy, at least quite cheerful, she thought, as she plunged her face into the water.

FOUR

WHEN Sara had helped Dad to fry sausages for lunch and cleared the table and washed up, she went outside and sat down on the steps of the veranda.

Dad had some important drawings to finish, and then in a few hours' time they would go to town. First they were going to Dad's office, then they would go and fetch Mother, and after that they would have dinner at Skansen.

As Sara sat there on the steps looking around with her eyes red from crying, she heard the airplane that always flew over at about this time. She raised her head and squinted at the sun, and her eyes hurt in the strong light. She recognized the large jets, and she knew that they carried passengers from the south—possibly from Rome or Paris. "I wonder who is sitting up there in the plane," she thought, and that reminded her of her own canceled trip, and disappointment began to gnaw at her again. Of course it was great to be going to town with Dad—yes, of course it was—and to have dinner at Skansen—that certainly would be fun.

But even so, the pleasant thought of the evening's enjoyment grew pale and disappeared, and all the unhappy thoughts returned like a swarm of blackbirds and grabbed her with their claws.

Sara sat there kicking the gravel so that the toes of her new red sandals got scratched and dirty. The cat Laban came up and rubbed against her legs to tell her that he wanted to sit on her lap, but she took no notice. A wagtail was playing about gaily on the garden path, but Sara looked the other way. And when the postman delivering the afternoon mail waved and said hello, Sara didn't even smile.

"Soon there won't be anyone left around here to deliver letters to," he shouted cheerfully. "Aren't you going away to the country soon?"

This wasn't exactly a good question to ask Sara at that moment, but of course the postman couldn't know.

"No," Sara replied sourly. "I'm not going to the country."

"Lena and Lasse and Anita and the others have gone already, I think," the postman said as he got on his bicycle again. "Cheerio!"

"Cheerio . . ."

That was the worst of it. There was not a single one of her friends left in the block called Sunrose, where

Sara lived. Her best friend, Lena, from across the road, had left even before the end of the term. Soon there would only be grownups left in all the houses round about, old people who worked or who were so old that they didn't work any more. Besides, even they went away. Even Lasse's grandmother, who would give you a glass of lemonade occasionally, had gone off in a taxi yesterday. And their nearest neighbors of all simply didn't exist. The large house that shared a hedge with them had been empty for more than a year.

If only the Holmgrens had still been there! Then it wouldn't have mattered, not going to the country.

What fun she had had with Pyttan and Loffie and Roffie and Kajsa and their fat mother, who painted peculiar pictures, and their thin little father, who sold shoes! They would never have such wonderful times in Sunrose again!

"They'll never sell that old ruin of a house," the neighbors said when the Holmgrens left with the moving van. And they were right—the house had been empty since last autumn, deserted and silent with blank windows for eyes.

At least, that is what Sara thought.

"Sara! Where are you?"

It was Dad's voice from the balcony. "Be a good girl and get me a packet of John Silver cigarettes from the corner store," he shouted, waving a piece of paper money. "You can buy yourself ice cream as well!"

Sara almost rushed straight into the enormous moving van standing outside the open gates of the house next door. Two men were carrying a large cupboard up the garden path. Apart from that, nobody was about. But if furniture was arriving, people must be coming, too!

Sara was so excited by the thought that at last someone was coming to live in the poor old empty house on the other side of the hedge that she almost forgot the errand for Dad. She stayed by the gate for a long time hoping to catch a glimpse of the new neighbors. But all she saw was the moving men, who came out again to get more furniture and boxes.

Finally she felt she ought not to stand there any longer.

Like a flash of lightning, she rushed down the road, then up the hill and around the corner by the bus stop, up to the store.

"A packet of John Silvers, please," she said, panting. She took the cigarettes and the change and hardly had time to say thank you to the friendly "man in the box," as the children used to call him.

"Don't you want ice cream today, Sara, since it's so hot?" he called after her.

"Haven't got time, haven't got time," she shouted, and ran off in a cloud of dust.

"Daddy, Daddy, some people are coming to Villa Valborg," she shouted from the stairs, which she mounted in three enormous jumps.

"Really?" Dad exclaimed, taking off his glasses. "So he managed to sell the house after all. I expect he had

29

to drop the price quite considerably. I wonder who the people are? I hope they are pleasant."

"Oh, I do hope they have children! I've only seen the moving men, but perhaps the others are inside the house. The truck was from Västerås, so perhaps that's where they come from. Now where is Västerås again? Oh yes, I know. Oh, Dad, how super this is!" Sara jumped up and down in her excitement. "Do you think . . . couldn't I go and see them . . . ask if I can help or something?"

Without waiting for a reply, Sara rushed out of the room and down the stairs.

"Take it easy, Sara. I'm sure they'd like to be left in peace," Dad called after her, but she didn't hear him.

The large moving van was practically empty when Sara got back, and the men came out of the house with their tarpaulins and ropes and prepared to leave.

"Hello there," one of the men said when he saw Sara standing by the fence. "Now you'll be getting some neighbors. That's good, isn't it?"

"Are they in there?" Sara asked timidly.

"No, they'll be arriving later from Tehran, or whatever it's called, out there in Persia. We have just brought their furniture that was stored in Västerås. You see, he used to work there, the engineer, that is. I expect they'll be here any moment now."

Any moment—that sounded promising.

But a moment can be terribly long. Sara felt that she had been sitting in the shrubbery waiting for hours before she heard a taxi driving along the road. She had it all worked out: as soon as she heard the car, she would creep around behind the house and position herself by the old peephole in the hedge—the peephole that in the old days of Pyttan, Loffie, Roffie, and Kajsa had been large enough to crawl through when one was in an awful hurry and didn't have time to go the roundabout way through the gate.

However, Sara hadn't allowed for the fact that the next-door garden had become terribly overgrown while the house was empty and no children played around among the bushes. The peephole had almost closed up, and the view was obscured by half-grown maple shoots and a tangled brushwood of hazel. Sara heard voices and footsteps and glimpsed some people walking past. Before she had been able to make out how many they were or what they looked like, they had disappeared through the front door. With a slamming of doors and a crunching of gravel, the taxi disappeared down the drive.

"Bother!"

Sara kicked at a thistle, which was doing no harm by the side of the hedge. "Bother! Soon we'll be going to town, and perhaps I shan't see them in time to tell Mother all about them."

Sara crept back into her own garden and sat down on the grass to think. Surely they would come into the garden after a while! At the moment they must be looking around the house, of course, but when they had done that, surely they would want to see the garden. If only she could think of some reason for walking past just then! Perhaps she could pretend that she was going to buy that ice cream.

If she stayed near the hedge, she would most certainly hear their voices when they came out of the house, and then she would rush out of the gate and walk slowly past their house without turning her head.

Sara lay down on her back and gazed up at the sky.

After that she sat up, picked a blade of grass, and folded it up and put it in her mouth. Then she took it out and looked at the mirror formed on the grass by her saliva.

Then she threw that away and began to look for four-leaf clovers in the grass. But she didn't find any.

She thought of going indoors to get something to eat, but decided it was too risky to leave her place in case the neighbors were to come out just at that moment.

Then she helped a green beetle that had fallen on its back.

Then she looked at a yellow butterfly perched on a flower, opening and closing its wings.

Then she lay down again and looked up at the sky.

Then she fell asleep.

The sound of voices close at hand woke her up—strange voices, on the other side of the hedge.

"Come and look here. What a lovely little playhouse, but there's a padlock on the door, so we can't get in because I haven't had the key yet," a woman's voice was saying. Sara thought she sounded young and cheerful. But whom was she talking to? Sara sharpened her ears so much that she felt they ought to stand up like a rabbit's—she was so anxious to hear the answer of the person the woman was talking to.

Surely it must be a child—and most probably a girl, although Roffie and Loffie had often played with the girls in the little house.

But why did she say nothing? Wasn't she pleased to have a proper playhouse? Or was she perhaps so terribly pleased that she couldn't say anything? That does happen sometimes.

"Look, we can peep in through the window here. I'll lift you up so that you can see better. Oh, there's a real little stove that you can cook things on and two little red chairs. How nice of them to leave the furniture, don't you think? And they've even left the curtains!"

Still no reply. What a strange girl!

Suddenly Sara felt so curious that she almost crept out of her skin. And before she had had time to think, she was on her way through the hole in the hedge.

Down there in the shade she stopped and crouched on all fours like a bloodhound, listening with her whole body. It was nasty down there in the undergrowth with sticks and twigs all over the place. She had pine needles in her hair and cobwebs over her face. But Sara had no time to take any notice of that.

Footsteps were retreating across the lawn—they could hardly be heard in the soft grass, but she felt the vibrations in the ground.

Then suddenly a man's voice was heard from the

33

balcony. "Margareta, do you know where I might find some thumbtacks?"

"I'm coming," the person called Margareta replied. "We have just been looking at the playhouse."

Who was "we?"

Sara waited a few more minutes, but there was neither movement nor sound from the other side, so she got up cautiously and stepped out into the sunshine on the neighbor's lawn.

She was quite dazzled by the light and just stood there looking around. The garden was deserted. The balcony and the veranda were empty, but voices could be heard from inside the house. She sighed and glanced at her watch. It would soon be time for her to go home and get ready. They were leaving in half an hour.

As she was moving slowly and stealthily back toward the hedge, she suddenly caught sight of the girl.

She was sitting on the little seat outside the playhouse, kicking her legs. Ooohh! Sara stopped abruptly and just stared. She felt she had never seen anyone so beautiful—one of those girls who don't exist in real life, only in fairy tales, films, and pictures.

Jet-black hair, dark almond-shaped eyes with long eyelashes like a doll's, thick dark eyebrows that almost met, a long, fine nose, and a red mouth.

Without thinking Sara put her hand up to her own face and pinched the freckled snub nose that stuck up between her blue eyes.

But the girl looked thin and pale and perhaps a little sad.

34

Her dress was very pretty, though, and she was wearing a beautiful necklace.

"Hello," Sara said at last, taking a step forward. "Hello, my name is Sara, and I live next door. What's your name?"

No reply. Sara, thinking that the girl had not heard the question, repeated, *"What's your name?"*

Still no reply. Perhaps she didn't understand Swedish? But . . . then surely it was odd that the woman had spoken Swedish to her before?

"I asked what your name is! Surely you must have a name, for goodness' sake," she added a little impatiently.

But the girl shook her head. Suddenly she got up and ran toward the house.

"I not want to be called Mary!" she cried wildly and desperately. "I hate Mary, hate Mary. Ma has promised me a new name. . . ."

With that she was gone. Sara stood there as if stunned. She shook her head . . . perhaps she was still asleep in the grass, perhaps it was all a dream.

A girl without a name. Could such a person really exist?

FIVE

"THERE are cherries growing on the wall here, so I'd like this room," the girl whispered as she moved her hand across the torn wallpaper.

"Look what a huge bathroom," Margareta called out. "The bathtub is a bit rusty, but there is a window, and what a lovely view!"

"Oh yes, it's a pleasant enough house." Bosse sighed. "But it's going to cost an awful lot to put it in order."

"Yes, but it *is* yellow," Margareta interrupted, "and I've always wanted a yellow house, and look what a lovely garden we've got with lots of flowers and a play-house and a garage and everything. . . ."

"Oh yes, I know." Bosse smiled. "We really had no choice, and we were lucky to get a place at all after being abroad for so long."

"Well, I think it's a dream house," Margareta declared. "Just to have a place of one's own after all those furnished apartments and depressing hotel rooms— what does it matter if it is a bit shabby? Don't you think it's nice here, too?" She turned toward the girl who was still standing in the room where bunches of faded red cherries could be seen amid the stains and tears in the paper.

"A little girl must have had this room—don't you think so, Ma?" the girl said, pointing to a torn paper doll that was attached to the wall with a pin.

"And in here I should think two naughty, boisterous boys used to live!" Bosse muttered from the next room. "A cracked washbowl, holes burned in the linoleum, and knife carvings on the doorframe . . ."

However, Margareta and the girl were not listening. They were working out how pretty and comfortable the cherry room would be once it was redecorated. That is, Margareta did the talking. The girl stood silent, seriously and attentively watching Margareta's movements with her black eyes.

". . . and we'll put the dressing table here, don't you think, with a little round mirror and a bow right at the top? That will look pretty . . . and you must have a desk where you can keep your school books and writing things and paint boxes . . . and here—no, perhaps it would be better here—we'll put the chest of drawers and at that end a small bookcase. And I think we could hang up my old doll's house—you know the one I told you about. It's in the attic at my mother's house . . .

"And what about curtains?" she continued. "What kind of curtains would you like? White ones with frills or flowery ones?"

The girl did not reply, but a happy sparkle had come into her eyes. She went up to Margareta and snuggled against her.

"Now I become a proper Swedish girl, quite sure," she murmured.

"Yes, dear, a Swedish girl who speaks Swedish and who will go to a Swedish school in the autumn," Margareta replied, stroking her dark hair.

"And then I will have a real Swedish name, you have promise," the girl continued.

"You shall have the most beautiful name you can find," Margareta said with a smile. "And you certainly are lucky—not many children can choose the name they like. But come on, let's go and have a look at the garden!"

They went out onto the balcony together and leaned against the railing with its peeling dirty gray paint.

It was a mild day in June with clouds chasing across the sky and a gentle breeze fluttering the leaves of the birch trees.

Straight ahead was a tall hedge separating them from the neighboring garden, where a red house with white ornamentation around the roof could be glimpsed among some old apple trees.

By the gate, askew on its rusty hinges, was a thicket of honeysuckle, and the lilac at the corner of the house sent up waves of fragrance. The lawn was dotted with yellow dandelions, peeping up among last year's dead

leaves, and on the golden knob of the flagpole a black-
bird was singing at the top of his voice.

Bosse and Margareta stood with their arms around
each other.

"At last we are at home," Bosse murmured. "To
think that all this really exists!"

"It smells nice," the little girl said, sniffing the air.
"It smells . . . it smells of Sweden."

Margareta smiled and sighed. Her eyes were full of
tears. She was thinking of the country they had left—
the country where the girl came from—a country with
burning hot sunshine and freezing nights. She thought
of the mud, dry and hard as stone, of the fine dust that
filled your mouth and nose, the yellow steppe with
camel brush.

"It smells of earth and water and fresh green plants,"
she said, putting her hand on the girl's shoulder.

"And it also smells of coffee boiling over," Bosse said
suddenly, and rushed indoors. "I completely forgot I
had put it on!"

Soon they were all sitting in the shabby kitchen
drinking coffee and hot chocolate. Bosse had found a
wobbly old garden table and put it by the kitchen window. He and Margareta sat on a packing case, and the
little girl sat on a large stone jar turned upside down,
which they had found in the pantry. The linoleum on
the floor was cracked and bumpy. A leaking tap kept
dripping, drip, drip, drip, and a smell of damp and old
cooking came from the cupboards.

40

But the sun was pouring in through the dirty windows, Margareta had put two flowers in an empty beer bottle on the table, and there was a delicious smell from the hot drink in the cups.

"I am as hungry as a horse," Bosse said, helping himself to a ham sandwich out of a package they had bought at the airport.

"This spotty sausage is the best thing of all in Sweden," the little girl said, taking an enormous bite out of her sandwich.

"You just wait until you have tasted cabbage and meat rissoles and brown beans and pease pudding and little pancakes with red whortleberry jam and herring with new potatoes . . . and . . ."

"You sound so horribly patriotic that I feel quite sick." Margareta laughed as she poured out some more coffee. "Would you like some more chocolate?"

"Oh, no, I'm so full up." The little girl sighed. "And sleepy . . ."

"You go and lie down on the sofa in the sitting room while we finish our coffee," Margareta said as she lit a cigarette.

"Surely one has a right to be patriotic if one hasn't been home for two years and hasn't lived here properly for five," Bosse continued when the girl had left the room. "It really seems an eternity. . . ."

"But surely it's not only the food you have missed?" Margareta smiled.

"No, of course not, though I have missed that, too. But there are so many other things . . . like . . ."

"Smells," his wife suggested. "Like that damp smell of earth and grass. And the white evening light, and the friendly chatter of the taxi driver, and well-known voices on the radio . . ."

"And the intonation when people talk . . . you

know what they mean. And funny stories you have heard before . . . and the faces of old school friends that you meet. . . . You can say half a sentence, and people understand. Everything you recognize and know . . ."

"In other words, a place where you feel at home," Margareta said slowly. "That is, everything that our little girl has lost . . ."

"Everything that we shall try to give to her again," Bosse interrupted.

"I only hope that we shall be able to make her happy," Margareta replied, snuggling up to Bosse in his dirty shirt. "So that she really will forget her terrible experiences and not just push them farther and farther down into her soul. If only those nightmares would stop . . . though she doesn't seem to have had so many lately . . ."

"Now we really musn't sit here doing nothing," Margareta suddenly exclaimed after a little silence. "We had better do some unpacking so that we get something to eat and somewhere to sleep before tonight. I'll take care of the bags of bedclothes upstairs if you unpack these boxes. . . . Oh, you're back, darling. Couldn't you sleep after all?"

"No, I have too much airplane in my head," the little girl replied, "and when I shut my eyes, the sofa goes up and down."

"Then you can help me arrange things here in the kitchen," Bosse said, swinging a hammer. "It's almost

43

as though we were settlers in the Wild West. But at least we don't have to live in a tent in the garden."

"The Wild Vest?" the girl asked, staring at Bosse in surprise. "What is the *Wild Vest?*"

"Not *vest,* sweetie, *West.* It's a country you'll soon get to know through TV and films," Bosse replied, and put down what he was holding to show her more vividly how wild the West was.

When Margareta returned some time later to look for a broom, she found Bosse sitting astride a large suitcase, holding his pipe by the barrel as a pistol and shooting violently at an unknown enemy who had evidently slipped into the pantry. On his head was a folded newspaper that was meant to look like a cowboy hat.

"Bang, bang, bang!" he shouted.

"Bosse, what on earth are you doing? You'll frighten the child out of her life!"

"I like it Ma. It's fun!" the little girl shouted from where she was sitting on the drainboard, using the hammer as a revolver. "Bang—bang—bang!" she shouted, and her serious face looked radiant. "We are Wild Vest, Ma. They always do this, Bosse says."

"However did you invent *that* game?" Margareta asked.

"The child must learn about the amusements of the West." Bosse laughed. "So we might as well start straight away. As you can see, the Wild West is appreciated even by a daughter of the East. We have just driven a cattle thief under the refrigerator, and the sheriff is a crook, so we can't expect any help from

44

him. Come and join us, Margareta. You could be the stolen cow!"

"What an idea!" Margareta exclaimed. "I'll give you something for that!"

She chased him around the kitchen with a broom, and the little girl cowboy on the drainboard almost choked with laughter.

SIX

IT certainly was a lovely evening at Skansen Park with Dad and Mum—violin music and candy floss, the smell of flowers and pork chops, escalators and baby bears, and ice cream and evening sunshine over the city.

But even so . . . even so, Sara couldn't help thinking about the girl next door nearly all the time. Again and again she had described to her parents what she looked like—what dark eyebrows she had, how pale her cheeks were, although her skin was dark, what large eyes. . . .

And this very strange business of her not having a *name!*

"Mummy, why do you think she said she didn't want to be called *Mary?*" Sara asked several times between mouthfuls. Why should her name be Mary if she came from Persia as the movers had said, and where was

Persia, anyway, and what did it look like? Was that where Farah Diba lived? Sara had a picture of her somewhere.

"It isn't called Persia nowadays," Dad said. "The name is Iran, and Farah Diba does live there, and she is married to the Shah, who is their king."

"He sits on the Peacock Throne," Mother added. "I remember that from school."

"Are the peacocks alive?" Sara asked with interest.

"I should certainly think not!" Mother laughed. "As far as I can remember, the throne looked like an enormous baking tray on feet or an imperial bed made of gold and precious stones with peacocks carved at the sides of the head end. It is very impressive, anyway, and I believe some shah or other pinched it from India."

"I read an article about Iran some time ago," Dad continued, "and it said that the country used to belong mostly to some terribly rich landowners and the farmers were just their slaves, but now they are giving land to the people. The soil is terribly dry and hard to cultivate, and Persia is full of deserts and plateaus except by the coast, where it is marshy. To grow things, they have to lead the water in underground canals from the mountains down to the plains," Dad continued.

"Don't they have a lot of earthquakes, too?" Mother asked. "There was an awful catastrophe some years ago. I remember reading about it, when thousands of people were killed and lost their homes."

"Are their houses like ours?" Sara asked. She was like blotting paper when it came to absorbing facts.

"Sometimes, in the large towns, but in the country

they build their houses out of clay and sand with large timbers to hold up the roofs, and as the last earthquake happened during the night, lots of people were killed because the roofs fell in. If you are out in the open, earthquakes are not so dangerous, you see."

Sara listened, wide-eyed.

"Are there never earthquakes in Sweden?" she asked.

"No, the strange thing is that they occur at definite places along a certain belt, and people know where those belts run. Turkey and Persia are the countries where earthquakes occur most frequently."

"Have we any books about Persia?"

"I doubt that very much," Mother replied. "But I think there is an old book from my childhood by Sven Hedin—you know, the explorer who wrote *From Pole to Pole*. I'll try and find it for you tomorrow morning before I go to town. But it's very old-fashioned and probably rather difficult for you to read."

"I'll manage," Sara replied confidently.

Being the youngest in the family, Sara was used to books being read aloud by her brothers and sister, and she was not put off by difficult sentences or words that she did not understand.

So early the following morning she was sitting up in bed with a splendid, large book with a white, blue, and gold binding. The title was *The Mission of King Oscar to the Shah of Persia* and it had been printed in the year 1890.

Sara carefully wiped her hands on the top sheet—

48

she'd had breakfast in bed as a treat—and then placed her index finger under the first word of the first line of the first chapter and began to read.

"Who has not in their younger days heard one of the thousand tales from Persia with their glowing descriptions of Oriental nomadic life, exciting adventures, hidden treasures, bewitched princes, and strange occurrences; who has not at some time or other heard stanzas from a Persian poem which tell of the blessed realm of Iran, that country more favored by Allah than all others, and its inhabitants, most blessed of all created beings, who would not for all the gold in the world exchange their homeland for another?"

Whew! "What a long sentence," Sara thought, "and even that isn't the end—just a lot of beastly semi-colons."

". . . and who has not many a time heard of the high snowclad mountains and the streams precipitating their water in foaming cascades . . ."

"No really, this is too hard." Sara sighed. And all that business about bewitched princes and hidden treasures and the rest she had read about in *A Thousand and One Nights*.

She skipped a section and then decided to give Sven Hedin a last chance.

"Dad," she called out a few moments later to her father who was in the bathroom shaving. "Dad, what does *insignia* mean?"

"What on earth are you talking about?"

"And what is the *Order of Serafin?*"

"It's some ornamental junk with a wide blue ribbon that kings and ministers and archbishops and people like that hang around their necks. But why on earth are you reading about that—I thought you wanted to find out about Persia?"

"Yes, but this is what it says in the book about Persia that Mother found for me. Sven Hedin had to take the Order of Serafin to the Shah."

"What a load of rubbish!" Father laughed. "Don't bother with all that! Even if you do learn something

50

from it, all that happened nearly eighty years ago, and Persia must look quite different these days. Why don't you get up and dress yourself and go over to the neighbors and ask them what Persia is like? Anyway, perhaps that moving man was mistaken—maybe they are not from Persia at all, but from Brazil or Tunisia or Afghanistan or some other country. And you will just have wasted your time learning all about Persia!"

"Yes, but, but . . . I'm too scared," Sara moaned. "Couldn't you come with me?"

"Now come off it. You don't really think I have time for that, do you?" Dad replied as he knotted his tie. "You weren't that scared yesterday when you crept through the hedge. Surely it's no worse today!"

"No, but you see, she seemed so frightened, and she doesn't answer when you talk to her. That makes me scared, too!"

"Of course she is shy and worried, arriving like this in a strange country—you would be, too. But she'll get over it. Anyway, we'll ask them all in one evening so that we can get to know each other. But meanwhile, you try to make a bit of contact! See you later!" With that Dad went into the room he used as an office and closed the door.

"Make a bit of contact!" That was easy enough for him to say. Surely she couldn't just stand by the fence and stare at them—or could she? Or ring the doorbell and ask if they would like to know where the shop was? Or ask if they, by any chance, had seen a gray cat with black stripes and three white paws? Yes! That was it!

51

They couldn't know that Laban was scared stiff of strangers and would never dream of visiting other people's houses.

Sara jumped out of bed and rushed to the bathroom. Nightdress off, a splash of cold water over her face, three strokes with the toothbrush, two with a comb, and then back to get her clothes. In two minutes she was ready.

She was halfway down the stairs when she heard Dad's voice.

"Sara, have you made your bed?"

"Oh no, I quite forgot . . ." Back again up the stairs. A quick pull at the bottom sheet, a shove at the pillow; the main thing was to get the blanket fairly smooth—then on with the coverlet and out again.

On her way Sara stumbled over the new green bag that still stood there packed and ready with bathing things and books to read on the journey. She kicked it to one side. Strange that yesterday morning seemed so long ago . . .

Then she had a sudden thought and went back to the bathroom to find her red hairband. She had better comb her hair properly so that she would look really nice. She even cleaned her nails before she left the bathroom, to complete the good impression.

A few moments later Sara, looking neat and tidy, rang the bell of the house next door. It seemed strange to be standing there ringing as she had done so many times before when the Holmgrens used to live there. It was pleasant to hear the loud clattering noise of the bell that Mrs. Holmgren said was noisy enough to waken the dead.

Sara's heart was thumping violently.

It was some time before she heard any movement inside. A woman's voice called out, "Bosse, there's someone ringing the doorbell. It sounds as though the house were on fire. Who on earth can it be at this early hour?"

Alarmed, Sara looked at her watch. It was ten past nine; surely that's not early? But . . . perhaps people in Persia had different habits . . . perhaps it was best for her to slip away quietly before anyone came to open the door. . . . What if they were terribly angry? She had only got halfway to the gate when the door was opened and a tall man in a striped dressing gown appeared on the step.

"Did you ring the bell?" he asked, smiling in the middle of a yawn. "You'll have to excuse us, but it was very late last night before we had unpacked and got to bed. Was there anything special you wanted?"

"Yes . . . well . . . that is . . ." Sara's mind was a complete blank—then suddenly she remembered. "Yes, you see, the thing is that our cat Laban is lost . . . and I . . . well, I wondered . . . if perhaps he had come in here?" Sara's face was bright red with the effort of making up this story.

"What does he look like?" the man in the dressing gown asked with a twinkle in his eye.

"He is gray," Sara replied promptly. "With black stripes down the sides and three white paws, and the

53

tip of his tail is also white, and one of his ears has a nick in it and . . . "

"Then that must be the cat sitting behind you by the gate," the man said gravely. "He certainly fits your description."

Sara swung around in a flash. Her rosy cheeks were scarlet. "Darn the cat," she thought. "Why did the wretch have to creep out like that and sit down and not look the slightest bit lost!"

"Oh, I'm most awfully sorry. He . . . he must have . . . he must have come back just now," she said, and rushed toward the gate.

"Hi, wait a moment," the man called after her. "Why don't you come in and meet our little girl? We were just about to christen her. Perhaps you could help!"

SEVEN

SARA remained standing doubtfully on the bottom step of the shabby old veranda. The man in the striped dressing gown had already disappeared.

What was that he had said? "We are just about to christen our little girl. Perhaps you could help!"

Sara knew exactly what happened at christenings. Only last spring she had gone with Father and Mother to the christening of one of Aunt Ingrid's grandchildren. Sara knew that it was an elaborate affair with a clergyman, a font, candles, wine, and biscuits. The child must be a baby in a long lace gown with a golden locket around its neck.

A christening was certainly not something you went to early one summer morning dressed in a striped dressing gown! And the child was as big as Sara herself—surely she should have been christened long ago by rights.

Sara felt worried. What if there was something strange . . . something really *weird* about the new neighbors? The little girl had been so odd yesterday—and now this business of Sara's coming in to help with the christening!

For a moment Sara felt like running away from it all, but finally her curiosity won, and she began walking up the steps slowly and cautiously. She stepped into the hall, which was as familiar as their own at home. It was full of empty boxes, bookcases, and chairs stacked on top of each other.

"Hello, there!" It was the man in the dressing gown again, and his voice came from the kitchen.

"Come in . . . come in. Now what was your name again? Sara, jolly nice name . . . that's what my old cat used to be called. My name is Bosse, by the way. Now, what was I going to say. Oh yes, why don't you have some tea with us? I am just making it, and the others will soon be down. Sit down on that box for the time being."

The man put another cup on the wobbly garden table. "Now perhaps I ought to explain a little about this christening," he continued. "You see, well, it's a long story, which you will probably hear later, but briefly the thing is that our little girl is Persian. She was looked after by some American missionaries for a couple of years in an orphanage in Tehran where I have been working for some time. She was the only survivor in her family of that terrible earthquake they had some years ago."

"I know," Sara interrupted excitedly. "The houses were smashed, and the timbers fell down and killed people who were asleep."

"How do you know that?" He turned toward her with raised eyebrows. "You are much too young to remember!"

"My dad told me about it."

"I see. Well, that's good—then you know what it's all about. Anyway, they christened her when she got to that children's home, mainly because she certainly hadn't been christened before according to Christian rites—most Persians are Mohammedans, if you know what that is?"

"Yes, they are the people who have Allah Allah," Sara replied, feeling pleased that she was able to show off what she had learned from *A Thousand and One Nights*."

"You do know a lot!" Bosse smiled as he poured boiling water into the teapot. "They also christened her because the shock of the catastrophe had made her forget her own name. However much they asked her, she couldn't say what her name was.

"So they christened her Mary, just like that. But for some reason she hated her new name from the very beginning. Perhaps something in the christening ceremony frightened her; she couldn't understand what it was all about—maybe she thought it was some kind of witchcraft or magic with the prayers and the water.

57

You never know. Anyway, she never settled down with those kind missionaries. She grew thinner and sadder every day, although the doctor said that there was nothing wrong with her. Then we happened to meet the matron of the childen's home, and we mentioned that we so much wanted to take a foster child as we have no children of our own. She thought of poor little Mary at once, and eventually Mary came to stay with us. She was quick to learn, and after a few months she could speak Swedish quite well.

"We soon discovered that she disliked the name Mary. So we stopped using it and promised to give her a real Swedish name. But we never had time to choose one before we left Tehran, so we decided to do that when we got back here. Of course she can't get rid of Mary, but I think it's quite legal to add a name if you want to. So she and my wife have been sitting up in bed looking through lots of names all morning."

The man started cutting some slices of bread. "I think I can hear them coming downstairs now," he added.

Sara felt herself growing hot with excitement at the thought of meeting the girl again.

"Allow me to introduce Miss Sara, our neighbor, who has graciously accepted my invitation to take morning tea in our exquisite kitchen," Bosse said solemnly with a ceremonious gesture toward Sara.

"And this is my wife Margareta, physiotherapist, gymnast, and very charming in my opinion!"

"Hi, Sara," said the fair-haired young woman, hold-

58

ing out her hand. She was dressed in blue jeans and a turtleneck sweater.

"How do you do," Sara replied politely.

"And who this young lady is," Bosse continued with a smile, "I really couldn't tell you yet. Perhaps she is Kerstin or Barbro or Ingrid or Frideborg or Henrietta! Or possibly Gunborg or Linnea or Nanna?"

"Now don't be silly, Bosse," Margareta said, and sat down at the table while the two girls just stood there without saying a word.

Sara thought the girl looked even more like a fairy-tale child than before. She looked less tired, her cheeks were not so pale, and her dark hair was hanging loosely down to her shoulders.

"The choice is between Gunilla and Karin," Margareta told them. "What do you think, Sara?"

"Shouldn't she . . . shouldn't she decide for herself?" Sara stammered.

"Yes, but she likes them both just as much, so she finds it difficult to choose, you see."

"Well, if I . . . I mean . . . I like Gunilla best. It's a pretty name, I think. It sounds like a little bell." Sara blushed.

"Let's have Gunilla, then," the girl whispered, and hid her face on Bosse's shoulder.

"OK . . . OK, that's settled," he shouted. "I now have the honor of introducing our daughter Gunilla, hurrah, hurrah, hurrah!"

"Hurrah, hurrah, hurrah!" Margareta echoed, and put a flower behind the ear of the newly named Gunilla, who sat perched on the upside-down preserving jar, looking solemn and embarrassed but with a happy sparkle in her eyes.

"Well," said Margareta, "now this little ceremony is over and we've finished our tea, why don't you girls go

out into the garden and get to know each other. I found a key hanging on a nail here, and it says 'Playhouse' on the label. You could go and tidy up there if you like. But first, Gunilla, you'll have to get dressed."

"Oh yes!" Sara exclaimed. "That would be super!"

"Here is the key to your own house, Gunilla," Margareta said, holding out a large iron key.

But the little girl did not take it. Instead, she turned around quickly, as though Margareta had been talking to someone behind her.

"She's talking to *you,* Gunilla!" Bosse said, laughing.

"Ooooh!" She went very red. "I . . . I forgot . . . *I* am Gunilla . . . I am Gunilla . . . I am Gunilla, Gunilla, Gunilla!" she sang, and ran out of the kitchen.

EIGHT

ONE of the best ways for two little girls from different parts of the world to get to know each other must surely be to tidy up a playhouse together—on a sunny day in June with bees buzzing in the air and the first roses coming out in the garden.

Sara was already standing by the locked door peering in through the little round window when Gunilla came walking across the bumpy lawn with the rusty old key resting on her open palm. She was singing, slowly and monotonously:

> "Now
> I am
> Gunilla, Gunilla, Gunilla—
> Now

I am
Gunilla, Gunilla, Gunilla—"

Sara suddenly realized that she did not know how old Gunilla was—she had forgotten to ask. Yesterday afternoon, when Gunilla sat on the bench outside and her face was sad and pale, she had looked at least fifteen years old. But now as she came along, singing as she walked across the lawn, her black eyes fixed on the key and a secret smile on her lips, she didn't seem more than seven or eight.

Sara was just about to ask her, but then she stopped herself, remembering what Bosse had told her. If Gunilla couldn't remember her name, perhaps she wouldn't know how old she was either. Anyway, what did it matter!

"*You* do it," Gunilla said shyly, holding out the key.

"No, no, *you* must," Sara protested. "After all, it's *your* house. It's not difficult at all. You just put the key in and turn it around. It's mighty crummy in there," she continued happily.

"What did you say?"

"It's might . . . well, I mean it is awfully . . . it is very dirty in there. They must have forgotten to clean up before they moved."

The playhouse, which had the splendid name "Teenie House" painted in blue and gold letters above the door, had once been quite a luxurious little place, with a room and kitchen where the ceilings were so high that

63

a visiting grownup could stand up straight. The little house originally had a different name when Mr. Holmgren, the shoe-shop man, moved in, but the name was soon changed to "Teenie House" after the eldest daughter Anna-Lisa, nicknamed Teenie.

"Now we must rename the house after you," Sara said, "but we'll leave that till the last. First we must clear up. I'll go home and get some cleaning things; then we shan't have to disturb Bosse and Margareta— anyway, they probably need the cleaning things themselves. You come along, and I'll show you our place. We'll nip through the hedge—it's quicker."

"Nip?"

"Yes, you see . . . we'll . . . what shall I say? . . . we'll creep through the hedge. Nip, that means you run or do something quite quickly."

So they nipped across to Sara's house, and Sara began to rummage in the cleaning cupboard.

"You take this bucket, and here is a rag and a scrubbing brush and some powder. I'll get some cloths and window-cleaning stuff and a broom, and we'll load them all onto the old wheelbarrow in the back garden."

When they had finished loading it, an upstairs window opened, and Sara's father leaned out.

"So there you are! I was beginning to think that you had vanished into thin air!"

"We were just going to come up and see you," Sara shouted as she laid a dustpan on top of the load on the barrow.

"This is Gunilla, and she has just been christened,"

Sara declared as she stepped into Dad's room and marched up to his desk, dragging the unwilling Gunilla behind her.

"He's not dangerous at all—the world's best dad, in fact!"

If Dad thought it a bit strange when he heard that Gunilla had just been christened, he certainly did not show it. He just got up and shook hands with the little girl.

"Welcome, Gunilla," he said with a bow, and Gunilla glanced hastily at Sara. Then she bent both her knees in an awkward attempt at a curtsy that looked so unfamiliar that Sara burst out laughing.

"Don't you curtsy when you meet people in Iran?" she asked, and Gunilla shook her head.

"Well, I think it was a very good Swedish curtsy," Dad said with a smile. "And, by the way, what are you two up to?"

"We're cleaning up the playhouse, and it's great fun, and we've come over here to fetch the cleaning things because it's mighty—"

"Crummy," Gunilla added for her.

"Aren't you clever," Sara said proudly. "Soon you'll be talking Swedish just like us! Now we really must push off."

"Don't forget to buy some milk before lunch," Dad said, and closed the door.

It is strange that it should be so awfully boring to make one's bed and tidy up in one's own room when it is such fun to scrub floors and clean windows in a playhouse!

First they had to sweep the floors. There were piles of dust and pine needles and dead leaves and old toffee papers in all the corners, and in the kitchen cupboard Sara found the most peculiar things—from a dead mouse and dirty doll's china to some stone-hard buns and an empty lemonade bottle.

"Smells like the plague in that cupboard," Sara remarked.

"The *plague?*" Gunilla looked terrified.

"No, no, not *really.*" Sara laughed. "That's what you say about nasty smells if something smells quite horrid."

At last it looked as bright as a house does after a really good spring cleaning. Sara had been home and searched out a piece of clean curtain from her mother's box of scraps, and Margareta had given Gunilla a flowered tablecloth and a little mat for the floor. There was paper on the shelves in the cupboard and flowers on the table. The windows sparkled in the sunshine. Of course the wallpaper was rather shabby, but that did not matter very much as Sara had torn some brightly colored pictures out of magazines and pinned them on the walls.

"This was my idol last year," she said, tenderly stroking the faded mop of hair in a picture of a pop singer. "Who was your idol?"

There was no answer.

"Don't you have an idol?"

Gunilla just shook her head.

66

She had no idea what an idol was, and she didn't want to ask.

"Oh, how stupid I am," Sara said with sudden embarrassment. "I quite forgot . . ."

While they had been working away at the house, Sara had more or less forgotten that Gunilla was not a Swedish girl.

Now as she sat on the steps of the playhouse waiting for Gunilla to bring Bosse and Margareta out to inspect their work, it occurred to her how strange it was that she knew nothing at all about Gunilla's life in her own country. "Please don't ask her anything about Iran," Bosse had whispered to Sara in the kitchen. "She doesn't want to remember . . ."

So Sara would never be able to ask, "What did your father do? What was your mother called? Did you have any brothers and sisters? Where did you live? What did you eat?" Or, "Did you go to school? Did you have any books, dolls, animals?"

"This afternoon we must have a housewarming party in your little cottage." Margareta's cheerful voice could be heard from the veranda. "You must ask Sara if there is a cake shop nearby . . ."

NINE

SARA sat on the edge of her bed in her underclothes dangling her legs. The sun had not set behind Villa Valborg, and the room was as light as in the middle of the day, but Sara was so tired that her whole body seemed to be humming. It had been a long and eventful day.

The party with cakes and fruit juice in "Nilla's Nest," as the house had been renamed after much discussion, was a great success. They had butter cake and cake with green icing from the French cake shop, and orange juice in paper mugs with straws to drink from, and ice cream to finish off with. Dad had dragged himself away from his drawings and calculations and joined them (he sat on the doll's stool), and Bosse had given a speech in which he said that they were *so* pleased that Sara lived next door and that Sara would help Gunilla to become a Swedish girl very quickly so that she could go to a Swedish school in the autumn.

Then Dad had given a speech, too, saying how *very* pleased he and Mother were that Sara had a playmate at last. Then he had explained about the twins' measles and the canceled trip to the West Coast, and then Margareta had said how lucky they all were, and they had drunk a toast to that. And Gunilla and Sara touched their paper cups together so violently that they spilled their fruit juice . . . and Gunilla had whispered to Sara that green cake was the thing she liked best of all the foods in Sweden—apart from salami sausage. And Sara had been as full of food as a boa constrictor when she trudged home with Dad—to cook supper!

She kept thinking about what Bosse had said about her helping Gunilla to become a Swedish girl.

She had asked Mum and Dad at the dinner table, "What *is* it actually to be a Swedish girl? Apart from speaking the language and so on?"

Mum and Dad exchanged glances.

"Well, it's difficult to explain, just like that," Mother replied.

"If you grow up in a certain country and you are surrounded by its scenery, if you speak the same language and read the same books and hear the same songs and go to the same kind of school and spend Christmas and summer holidays in more or less the same way as the people around you," Dad began to explain, looking thoughtful, "then I suppose you could say that . . ."

"But what can *I* do to make Gunilla into a Swedish girl as Bosse said?"

"You can play with her, teach her things, show her your books and toys," Mother suggested.

"But why doesn't she want to be a Persian girl? Surely that's much more exciting, with peacocks and golden thrones and jewels and all that. I'd love to know all about things there, but I don't dare ask Gunilla because she doesn't want to think about it."

"Yes, Bosse told me, when we were alone, that she still has terrible nightmares, and she never wants to talk about them afterwards," Dad continued. "Several doctors out there examined her, and they said that she hasn't lost her memory in the real sense. She simply does not *want* to remember; she pushes the memories away. They also thought that it might be some particular event connected with the disaster that is causing the trouble."

"Some terrible secret, you mean?" Sara asked.

"Exactly. And now Bosse and Margareta are hoping that once Gunilla settles down here in Sweden and feels secure and happy, all those dreadful memories will fade away. Or perhaps she might be able to tell someone what happened and become free of it in that way."

"Just like when you tell about something naughty you've done and feel quite light in your tummy afterwards," Sara added.

Sara looked around her room. She had not been in there except to sleep since Gunilla arrived, and she was quite surprised to notice her doll Ulrika, dressed in traveling clothes, still sitting on her chair, staring in front of her.

71

She looked rather reproachful, Sara thought, as if she were saying, "Here I sit, completely forgotten, with my hat and coat on day in and day out, without even sleeping in my own bed at night."

And the worn old teddy bear, who had fallen under the chest of drawers, seemed to be muttering the same kind of thing when Sara picked him up and brushed the dust out of his fur—poor old Teddy who usually slept in Sara's bed with the monkey Johanna and Mother's old washed-out cardigan!

Sara staggered up and hurriedly put Ulrika and Teddy to bed. Ulrika had to put up with going to bed with all her clothes on—it couldn't be helped. *If only she were in bed herself!* But she was too tired to go and wash herself and clean her teeth. Of course her knees looked terrible after the floor scrubbing—not to mention her feet!

She lay down on her back on top of the bedspread. Although the window was wide open, she didn't feel the least bit cold. The curtains fluttered gently; she could hear a mosquito buzzing near her ear, and from across the road came the sound of the Svensson's radio playing, "Yellow submarine . . . Yellow submarine . . ." On her wall was the latest photo of "The Hep Stars" stuck in front of a picture from an old fairy tale.

Sara thought dreamily about Gunilla in the house on the other side of the hedge. She was probably sleeping in Kajsa's old bed, counting the cherries on the wallpaper, perhaps; and tomorrow would be another fine sunny day, and they would play in the playhouse and

72

perhaps bake a real little sponge cake at home in the kitchen, and then Gunilla would go with her to the supermarket and do the shopping for Dad. They probably couldn't cycle as Gunilla had no bicycle, but perhaps she could borrow Annika's old one, that is, if she knew how to cycle—perhaps they had no bicycles in Tehran? And they would sit in the garden reading books, and if it got very hot, they would get Dad to blow up the rubber paddling pool on the lawn, and he could shower them with the garden hose; and in the afternoon Mother would be at home, and she could play all the old songs and nursery rhymes for Gunilla so that she would learn to be a real Swedish girl; and the best thing of all was that she had Gunilla as her very own friend, and she would teach her a lot of things and . . . and . . . and . . .

There she fell asleep. And so ended the first day of Sara's and Gunilla's life together, and it was the start of a very different summer holiday, which Sara would probably never forget in all her life.

In Villa Valborg Margareta was ironing curtains in the kitchen while Bosse was perched on a ladder fixing curtain rails. Every now and then one of them tiptoed upstairs and glanced through the open door of the room with cherries on the wallpaper where Gunilla was asleep. A covered night light that stood in a corner on the floor gave a soft glow, which was friendlier than the white summer's night outside.

As always Gunilla lay on her side with her legs drawn right up and her arms around her head as if to protect herself. Often she would call out in her sleep, muttering incomprehensible words in Persian and then fall into deep sleep again. Or she would sit straight up in bed with terror on her face, screaming. However, this particular evening she had slept unusually peacefully. Once when Margareta came up to have a look and leaned over the bed, she heard Gunilla murmur a few words that for once she could understand.

"Cake with green icing," she murmured, and turned over toward the wall. "Green icing . . ."

TEN

"TODAY we are going to play school, and I'll teach Gunilla a lot of useful things that she'll have to know by the autumn," Sara said eagerly to Mother and Father at breakfast.

She was so excited about her plans for the day that she didn't even have time to sit down at the table to eat. She stood up and chewed crispbread so that her ears crackled.

"I've been thinking about this all night," she declared. Mum and Dad, who knew how well she had slept, looked at each other and smiled.

"I must take a whole lot of things to the playhouse," Sara continued, gulping a mouthful of tea. "Please, Mother, could I borrow that little bell that's in the cupboard so that I can ring for the lessons to start and finish? And could I have some money so that I can buy some new exercise books at the paper shop? It's much more fun to have real exercise books, and all my old ones are full, anyway. Oh, and do you think Gunilla can write?"

"I'm sure she can. After all, she went to an American school with those missionaries. But perhaps she can't write Swedish very well, so you could give her some practice with her spelling. Of course she speaks quite well, but that's rather different. I don't suppose Bosse and Margareta have had much time to give her any writing practice."

"Oh, then we'll have dictation every day," Sara exclaimed delightedly, completely forgetting that dictation was one of the things she hated most. "I'll take my old reading book over there, and we'll sing hymns and do sums and scripture and have school dinners. Please, Dad, do you think you could manage to get your own lunch today? Then I could take sandwiches and yogurt to the playhouse, or perhaps we could have our meals outside in the garden!"

Sara jumped up and down with excitement.

"Well, I'll have to try and manage on my own then," Dad said with a grin. "Here is some money for school materials—and don't forget to buy some rolls when you go shopping."

An hour later lessons were in full swing in the third grade of the primary school at Nilla's Nest.

A more willing pupil than Gunilla would be difficult to find. She sat on a little red chair at the school desk

77

that Sara had made by laying a plank across two boxes. She sat with her hands folded in her lap and a serious expression in her large eyes. She was surrounded by the other pupils of the class. Sara felt that it was far too lonely to have only one pupil, and with combined efforts the girls had managed to fill the classroom with a varied but silent company.

Next to Gunilla was Anna-Lisa. She was Gunilla's new doll, dressed in national costume. On their first day Bosse had gone into town and bought her. She was as tall as a two-year-old child, and she wore a costume with a striped apron and a little pointed hat.

When Sara first saw Anna-Lisa, she felt green with envy. Then she remembered that she also had one of those huge dolls, who sat upstairs in a cupboard with her china-blue eyes staring from under thick, dark eyelashes. The doll had been given to Sara by an aunt of her father's whose name was Sara, too. That was at Christmas three years ago. For the first few days Sara was quite overjoyed at possessing such a large, beautiful doll with patent leather shoes and a green satin dress and long, silky blond hair. Poor old Ulrika lay about forgotten and neglected.

For about a week Sara lived only for Katarina, as the doll was called. But soon—Sara didn't know herself quite how it came about—her love cooled off. Katarina was simply too large and too beautiful. You had to be careful with her all the time, and she was impossible to have in bed. Sara tried several nights running, but Katarina kept falling out of bed, and every time

78

Sara turned over, the doll cried "Mama" in a most piti-
ful voice.

"Katarina stops me from sleeping at night," Sara
complained. "She is too big. Of course, it's fun to *have*
big dolls, don't you think, Mother? But they're not
quite so good for playing with."

Mother agreed with her.

Sara could tell from the expression on Gunilla's face
as she came dragging her enormous Anna-Lisa that in
her heart of hearts she felt the same. But in a class at
school, of course, they were very useful. So now the
two huge ladies, Anna-Lisa and Katarina, each sat on
a red chair looking splendid in their beautiful clean
clothes, staring with their large, stupid eyes. Ulrika sat
in the second row with a stool for a desk, and her little
black peppercorn eyes looked quite intelligent com-
pared with the eyes of the big girls. Teddy looked quite
lively, too, although it was evidently quite a strain for
him to keep his floppy body upright and not let go of
the pencil Sara had given him.

On the doll's stove the cat Laban was asleep. Sara
had tried to make him sit up straight on the little chest
of drawers and attend to the lesson, but he flatly re-
fused. As soon as she let go of him, he leaped up onto
the stove and settled down with his head on his paws.

Teacher sat at the red table by the window, with a
ruler, an eraser, three pencils, and a pile of books. A
pair of dark glasses, much too big, were perched on her
little snub nose, and her short braids were pulled into
a knot on top of her head. Next to her on the wall hung

her sister Annika's old blackboard, cracked and gray with age, and also a picture of an oddly shaped chicken clambering out of an Easter egg and a torn map of one of the counties of Sweden.

Teacher Sara had just sung a hymn in a loud and clear voice and was setting her class to do dictation.

"No talking, now, Katarina," she said severely, "and Teddy, you really must *try* and hold your pen. . . . What is it, Ulrika—go to the toilet? Why didn't you think of that during recess? Now pay attention, and we'll start our dictation." Gunilla was the only one who was not told off at all. With an almost joyful expression on her face she was slowly writing down the words that Sara was reading in her new pale blue exercise book. As she wrote, her tongue moved, from one corner of her mouth to the other.

"The beaver is really an interesting animal. His length is more than half a meter, and he has a long, powerful tail. He lives on the bark of trees and certain kinds of roots."

Sara read this out very loud, as though she thought that Gunilla was deaf. And Gunilla wrote with her tiny fiddling handwriting, which was so different from the one Sara learned at school.

"The beever is a reely intresting annimul. His lenth is more than harf a meeter and he has along parfull tale. He lives on the baak of trees and surtn kainds of rutes."

"Oh dear," Sara exclaimed as she leaned across to look at what Gunilla had written. "How silly I am! I

80

had quite forgotten how difficult things like 'half' and 'bark' are to spell. I found it hard, and after all, I *am* Swedish!"

"I am Swedish, too," Gunilla said, looking so miserable that Sara was afraid that she would burst into tears. "I want to learn to spell properly!"

"I'm sure you will, *terribly* quickly," Sara comforted her hastily. "It's my fault, too, you see, because I speak with such a Stockholm accent, Dad says, and Stockholmers get lots of their sounds mixed up, and he's quite ashamed of me as he comes from the Southwest. . . . Now you must *copy* from a book instead, and then you'll see what the words look like. Meanwhile, the others can do mental arithmetic so they don't disturb you. Now listen, children, open your arithmetic books and turn to page eight. . . . Gunilla, here is a book with pictures—it's more fun!"

Silence fell in the classroom again.

The June sunshine poured in through the tiny windows of the house and made a pattern of squares on the floor. Specks of dust danced in the beam of light, and flies buzzed against the windowpanes. Teacher pushed her glasses up onto her forehead and rested her chin on her hands. Laban opened his greeny yellow eyes and looked as thoughtful as if he, too, were doing mental arithmetic.

In the midst of this sleepy silence Gunilla sat writing, her lips pursed determinedly and her dark eyebrows drawn together in a frown.

"Once there was a cat, an ordinary gray pussycat

with a pink nose and pink pads on his paws. The sad thing about this cat was that he had no tail."

Sara sat watching Gunilla and dreaming about Persia, and she thought how strange it was that Gunilla did not want to tell anything about her country. . . . And this peculiar business about her name. Did she really know deep down inside her what her name was? And what was the nasty secret that made her want to forget?

Sara wished that a magic carpet like the ones she had read about in fairy tales would come and take her to Persia so that she could find out what it was like. And she would see if it really was true, as Bosse had told Dad, that you could see children faint in the streets of Tehran because they had not eaten for a long time, and people would walk past without taking any notice. And little girls her own age would have to sit all day making carpets until their backs grew quite bent.

Thud!

Laban jumped down from the stove and roused teacher from her dreams.

"Oh," Sara exclaimed. "Is that the time? Then we must have a break." She got out her little bell and rang and rang. "Come along children, we must go to the dining hall," she called, and skipped out through the door.

Gunilla, who was rather reluctant to drag herself away from the story about how a mouse had bitten off the tail of the gray cat, followed her slowly with a thoughtful expression on her face.

"Dining hall?" she said rather anxiously.

"Oh, where we eat of course—school food, food that you have at school during recess. I wonder what we'll be having today?"

"Don't you *know* what you are having?" Gunilla sounded surprised. "I thought you always had yogurt and sandwiches?"

"Of course I know." Sara giggled. "I was only pretending. At school we are always so curious to know what we'll be having, you see. That is, if we haven't had time to find out from the papers in the morning, because it always says in the paper what the meal will be. It's exciting to see if you get something nice like sausages with grated carrots or black pudding, or something nasty like boiled fish and vegetable soup."

"Black pudding?" Gunilla sounded alarmed. "What is it? Is it all horrible and black? Do you have to eat it?"

"It's delicious," Sara assured her. "With lots of whortleberries."

"What did you say? Whortle . . . whortleberries? What are they?"

"Don't you know what whortleberries are? I thought they grew all over the world—little red hard, shiny things that grow in the woods in September, and you boil them with lots of sugar in great big pans and keep them in stone jars in the cellar."

Gunilla shook her head without saying a word and

84

looked very dejected, as though it were her fault that whortleberries did not grow in Persia.

"Never mind, I'm just being silly," Sara said hastily. "Come along. Let's go and get our food, and we'll meet on the lawn under the apple tree."

ELEVEN

so the days passed, and each day Sara and Gunilla played together.

When the weather was fine, they played hide-and-seek and climbed trees and built huts in their gardens, or cooked pretend food on the stove in the playhouse, or played shop with sand for coffee and lilac leaves for spinach.

When it was rainy and windy, they went upstairs to the attic in Sara's house and dressed up in her mother's old balldresses and her grandmother's high button-up boots and ostrich-feather hat. Or they went to the hobby room in the cellar of Gunilla's house and played snakes and ladders or did jigsaw puzzles or read old comics or strummed on the old organ left behind by the Holmgrens.

Sometimes they went to town with Margareta and bought clothes for her and Gunilla in the summer sales, and sometimes Sara's mum and dad would take them for Sunday outings in the car. When Mother had an afternoon off, she would sing songs with them at the piano, and sometimes Bosse read stories to them in the garden. Occasionally in the evenings they watched TV.

It was no longer necessary for Sara's dad to work at home to look after Sara and keep her company. Instead, Sara had lunch in the kitchen at Villa Valborg whenever she and Gunilla were not having a picnic in the garden or "school dinners" outside the little playhouse. Bosse and Margareta were both on holiday until the first of September, and they were spending the time fixing up Villa Valborg. Of course they could not do everything themselves, but they managed quite a few odd jobs while they were waiting for carpenters, painters, and plumbers to arrive.

Midsummer came and went.

The weather was really fine, for once, and Margareta helped the girls to decorate a little doll's maypole in front of the playhouse with birch leaves and garlands of buttercups and other wildflowers. Then they danced around the maypole with dolls and teddy bears and sang all the traditional midsummer songs. In the end the dancing grew so wild that Teddy's sawdust began to run out, and Katarina lost her eyes! In the afternoon the girls went with the grownups to Skansen to see the giant maypole there and all the boys and girls in national costume dancing and singing.

"You'll never find anything more Swedish than this," Bosse said to Gunilla as they strolled slowly home up the garden path in the white evening light.

All the roads and gardens were deserted and silent, except for the faint sound of a transistor radio some distance away. But the pop singers did not manage to drown the sound of the thrush trilling from the branches of the big pine tree in the garden of Villa Valborg. The honeysuckle growing around the shabby old veranda sent out its perfume of vanilla and honey, and the white blossoms of the lilac stood out like plumes of feathers against the green background of leaves.

Gunilla sat down on the bottom step and sighed.

"Are there no *stars* in Sweden?" she asked a little plaintively, looking up at the midsummer sky.

"Of course there are," Bosse replied, "but it's so light, you see, that they are not really visible. But you can usually see Venus blinking away somewhere above the treetops. Yes . . . there it is."

However, Gunilla was not very impressed even when she saw the reddish light of Venus as it could be glimpsed above the shed of the house next door. Bosse and Margareta understood that Gunilla was thinking of another starlit sky, a sky like a dark blue icy-clear sparkling dome above the dry Persian plains.

"Oh, if only," Margareta thought, and the anxiety she constantly felt about Gunilla caught hold of her and brought sudden tears to her eyes, "if only we could talk naturally about the past . . . if we could only say, Gunilla, do you remember . . . do you remember . . ."

"You just wait until August," Bosse was saying. "Then you'll be able to see stars . . ."

Wait, wait . . . Margareta felt that they had been waiting for so long now, waiting for something to happen—something that would release their little girl from the spell she was under, just like a princess in a fairy tale. Something—but what?—that would dissolve the sad memories and stop the terrible dreams that kept coming, although less frequently than before.

They had hoped so eagerly that all would be well as soon as they got back to Sweden.

Margareta stood on the veranda steps and looked down at Gunilla's face, dark, beautiful, mysterious in the fading light. Her cheeks had grown rounder and rosier lately, but her eyes were as guarded as ever, constantly keeping watch over a secret, it seemed.

"Now, what I really would like is a nice hot cup of tea," she exclaimed, interrupting her sad thoughts, shivering a little in her thin summer coat. "Come on, Gunilla, let's go in before we catch cold!"

"Tea with cinnamon buns," Gunilla said with longing in her voice, and her foreign accent was almost gone.

And so the days went by, and the girls continued to play. With each day Gunilla's Swedish improved. She learned to put the words in the right order, and she learned to pronounce difficult words correctly.

She responded to the books in Sara's bookcase with tremendous enthusiasm, and although she still read very slowly, she would sit for hours working her way through a book.

She got to know all the stories that Swedish children love, and she also learned to sing all the old songs and nursery rhymes. Before many weeks had passed, she could also tell which records were at the top of the pops!

With each day that passed, there was less need for Gunilla to ask Sara, "What's that?" They played and

90

played all day long, and Sara felt that she had never had a nicer friend in all her life.

But one evening when Mother came up to say good night, she noticed that Sara did not look very happy.

"What is the matter, darling?" Mother asked. "Is something upsetting you?"

"I just long for the Holmgren children—and Lena and Lasse and Anita," Sara whispered, and hid her face on Mother's shoulder.

"Do you really?" Mother sounded rather surprised. "I thought you had such fun with Gunilla every day!"

"We do have fun," Sara continued, trying to stop her voice from trembling. "We have terrific fun, but sometimes I get so *tired* in a way. It's so tiring to be kind all the time . . . to remember . . . to remember that you have to feel sorry for her always . . . that you mustn't quarrel or lark about or tease her . . ."

"I understand," Mother said, sitting down on the edge of the bed. "It is difficult, even for grownups. But listen, I really think that you should try to forget that you have to feel sorry for her—just be quite natural with her and treat her like one of your other friends. Gunilla will never fit in with her new life here if everyone keeps treating her in a special way because they feel sorry for her. Really, people don't want to be pitied, you know. It becomes a burden to them. Of course, you mustn't be nasty to her," Mother continued, "and you must help her as much as possible, but try not to think: *Now I must be kind, I must be kind, I must feel sorry for her.*"

"Yes." Sara sighed. "But it's so difficult not to, because . . . because she never says anything about herself and about Persia and her mother and father. She laughs and enjoys herself when we play, but all the time it's as if . . . I don't quite know how to explain it . . . all the time it seems as if she were really somewhere else, or as if she . . . were locked up in a cage or something. Do you see what I mean, Mother?"

"Yes," Mother replied. "I think I know what you mean, and I believe that Bosse and Margareta feel just the same. You know that they do all they can to make her feel safe and happy here in her new country with her new family. I think they were hoping that things would change as soon as they got back here and Gunilla got away from that missionary home where she was so unhappy. But the past still seems to be too strong for them—in spite of all their care and despite the fact that Gunilla herself is trying so hard to feel at home. But I have heard that they are planning to take her to a new doctor," Mother continued. "Unfortunately everyone is on holiday now, so they have to wait until later on. So for the time being, it's just a question of being patient."

"Perhaps it's terribly tiring for Gunilla, too, to go around like that with everyone being so frightfully kind to her, do you think, Mum? But of course, one can't decide to hit someone, just like that, because it might be good for them!"

"No," Mother agreed, "that would certainly make matters worse!"

Sara sighed, kissed Mother good night, and turned toward the wall with Teddy under her arm and the old pale-blue cardigan under her pillow.

In spite of her troubles, it only took a few minutes before she was asleep.

Every night she dreamed about Persia.

She dreamed of how she searched and searched for the secret of the forgotten name. She never knew quite when her daydreams became sleeping dreams, when the odd bits of knowledge about Gunilla's country that she had picked up from books and from Bosse and Margareta turned into fantasy pictures and fairy-tale dreams.

Sometimes she was a magician traveling on their flowered sitting-room carpet to a country with golden domes and ornate towers . . . a country of deserts and green oases . . . of gardens full of roses and watermelons and running streams . . . of mud huts and salty marshes and snowclad mountains.

The magician searched and searched for the magic formula stolen from him by a wicked dwarf—the formula with the mysterious words that would open the door of the cage where the silent blue bird was held captive . . . or the door of the high mountain where the princess was a prisoner.

Sometimes she was an explorer like Sven Hedin jogging across the desert in a sandstorm on the back of a weary camel.

The little brass bell hanging around the camel's neck tinkled and tinkled, and the halter was decorated with red and yellow tufts of wool. In the distance the sinister howling of jackals could be heard, but in the branches of the date palms nightingales were singing.

She was looking for a district where the earthquake raged, to find the remains of the village or town where Gunilla lived with her family. One evening just as the moon had risen, she found the right place, and she met a person who told her that Gunilla's parents were not dead at all, or perhaps it was only her old Granny who was still alive. Granny understood at once that Sara had come with greetings from her little grandchild, and Granny cried for joy and called her name again and again . . . a strangely beautiful name.

When she woke up, Sara had always forgotten it.

But the following night she went on persistently, riding on a dream donkey, and along the road there were teahouses where she went in. Women dressed in dark blue robes were rinsing clothes in ponds where goldfish swam. There were red flowers and plum trees and lilac bushes, and by the entrance to the house there was a curtain made of pearls, and inside there were men with black beards and stripey pajama trousers smoking water pipes that bubbled and gurgled . . . and they drank tea from glasses, and someone chopped sugar up with a little ax . . . and little boys played flutes, and someone hit a child so that it screamed . . .

Then she went around to everyone and asked and asked about the name, but they only laughed and laughed and told lies.

TWELVE

"ON Friday it will be Gunilla's birthday," Margareta told Sara one day when they were alone in the kitchen after lunch.

"So she remembers when her birthday is, then?" Sara asked in surprise.

"No, the thing is, nobody knows when she was really born or how old she is as all documents and papers were lost in the earthquake."

"But you said before that she was nine years old," Sara objected.

"Yes, that is what they thought at the children's home. They believed that she was five or six years when she arrived there, but of course, she was so thin and frail that it was hard to tell. All the children who were looked after there were given a new birthday on the day that they were registered with the authorities, and Gunilla's day was July 12."

"What fun having a birthday in the middle of the summer," Sara exclaimed. "At home we all have birthdays in the spring or round about Christmas. What are you giving her?"

"Aha, that's a secret that we are not letting anyone into, not even you!" Margareta laughed.

"How mean of you! Well, secrets are rather fun really." Sara stopped suddenly as she remembered the sad and burdensome secret of the lost name. "I mean, *short* little secrets are fun. Anyway, I think it's better not to know as it's so difficult not to tell anybody."

So on Friday Sara was as curious as the birthday child herself when she left home early in the morning with a package containing a book under her arm and a phonograph record in a paper bag. Margareta had asked her to wear a costume as they always used to dress up for birthdays at home when Margareta was a child.

A wicked little pirate with droopy moustaches drawn with burned cork, a kerchief tied around her head, and a black patch over one eye knocked rather timidly at the back door of Villa Valborg.

"Goodness, what a fright you gave me!" said the cowboy who opened the door, although he had a lasso over his shoulder and a pistol in his belt.

"You look splendid, Bosse," the pirate exclaimed, thumping him on the back, "although real cowboys never have beards."

"What do you think of me, then?" Margareta asked,

96

fluttering a fan as she laid violets and rose petals around Gunilla's new birthday cup, which had pink flowers on it and FOR A GOOD GIRL around the rim.

"Oh, how super! You're just like Carmen in the opera I saw last year, although your legs are not as fat as hers. Is that your own dress?" she continued enviously. "I'd love to have one like that to wear when I'm invited to fancy-dress parties at school. What a lot of frills and a real silk shawl . . . and that huge comb, though really your hair should be black. . . . But where is the *present?*" she suddenly broke off. "Shouldn't it be on the tray?"

"That would be a little difficult!" The cowboy giggled, picking up some matches to light ten little white and red and green candles that were placed in a ring in the center of the birthday cake that Margareta had made. It had yellow icing and was decorated with little grains of chocolate and pieces of candied fruit.

"But where *is* it?"

"Out there in the hall."

Sara turned around quickly and shot like an arrow through the kitchen door. She could see nothing. Oh yes, what was that over in the corner? It looked like an old-fashioned sewing machine or something, covered with a dust sheet right down to the floor. Sara went up to it and cautiously pulled the cover aside.

"Oh! A bicycle!" She went quite red under the soot of her moustache. That was the most wonderful present! Sara had to raise the black patch over her eye so that she could have a good look.

So shiny and new with gleaming red mudguards and

97

a hand brake and everything. Super! Now she and Gunilla could go out for rides—when Gunilla had learned to bicycle of course.

A moment later the colorful little group trooped up the worn old stairs, first the Spanish lady with a tray and candles, then the pirate with *Swedish Folktales* under her arm and a pop record in her hand, and last the Wild West man dragging the disguised bicycle.

A little girl with rumpled black hair opened her eyes wide in amazement at the sound of a strange song.

> "Happy birthday to you,
> Happy birthday to you,
> Happy . . ."

Gunilla sat bolt upright in bed, silent and serious, and stared at them as the door opened.

"You should be lying down with your eyes shut, Gunilla," Sara hissed at her in the middle of the singing, but Gunilla just went on sitting there with her mouth half open and her eyes wide with astonishment.

"Don't you remember that it's your birthday?" Sara asked.

"Many happy returns of the day!" Bosse and Margareta said. "We would like to present you with a little birthday gift which we hope will give you pleasure for many years. Pull the sheet off, Sara . . . abracadabra!"

Gunilla opened her mouth even wider, but she didn't say a word. Very, very slowly amazement gave way to pleasure, and Gunilla began to smile. Her eyes looked radiant.

"Oh," she murmured. "Is it mine . . . really mine? You are . . . so kind . . ." Suddenly she put her hands over her face and began to sob.

"But, Gunilla . . . come on, darling . . . you mustn't . . ."

"It's quite easy to cry when you're happy, too," Sara said sensibly. "At home we cry an awful lot when we're happy. It soon passes."

Of course Sara was right, and quite soon the two girls were busy with cycling lessons on the road: Gunilla perched on the saddle, holding on to the handlebars with a desperate grip, Sara trotting along behind holding more or less firmly onto the back of the saddle in the hopes of preventing the wobbly machine from crashing.

When Sara grew tired, Bosse and Margareta had to take over.

Gunilla counted eleven bruises, three bumps, a scratched knee, a torn skirt, and a sprained toe before, after three days, she could say proudly, "Now I can cycle!"

Since the girls could now go out for little bicycle trips, their days seemed to have a new and exciting purpose.

On the other side of the main road and the shopping center, there was a large empty area of land waiting to be built on. There were fields and meadows that used

99

to be part of a farm, and little groups of trees where wood anemones grew in the springtime, and round hillocks where you could ski in the winter. Little roads and peaceful footpaths ran across the area, and it was almost like being in the real country if you disregarded the tall houses round about and the water tower like a huge mushroom in the background.

When Sara's brothers and sisters were younger, they used to have marvelous games out there in Goldfield Park, as it was called, although it was not a park at all, really. But some years ago the rumor had spread among the children that a nasty man lived in Goldfield Park. Some people even said that they had seen ghosts there, and Lasse and Lena had sworn that there was a be-witched dog with a long tongue of fire that ran about at night, wailing like a wolf—Mr. Johanson in the co-op had told them, so there!

Because of all these silly rumors and fantastic stories the children were no longer very keen on going down to the park, except in the company of a grownup.

One Sunday Sara's mother and father had taken the girls for a long walk all over the park, and Sara could not understand why people had made up all those nasty, frightening stories about a place as nice as Goldfield Park, green and sparkling in the summer sunshine with its rough grass and beautiful trees.

Even the derelict old barn with swallows nesting under the roof looked friendly and inviting. Not a sign of nasty men or bewitched dogs as far as the eye could see! Only a young mother here and there sitting with her carriage in the shade of an overgrown apple tree, knitting or reading, or an old man from the old people's home enjoying a walk on the pleasant little roads.

Those quiet little roads were also very good to cycle on if you were just a learner, so Sara and Gunilla went for outings on their bicycles to Goldfield Park as soon as Gunilla felt confident on the road.

Outings—that lovely word, meaning things like hard-boiled eggs and nicely packed sandwiches, salt wrapped up in tiny pieces of paper, fruit juice in bottles with clip-on corks, and plastic plates from older brothers' and sisters' scouting days.

Outings—that meant finding old rucksacks in the attic and old blankets in the cupboards. It meant making nice little parcels out of grease-proof paper and not forgetting the egg spoons and the paper napkins and the comics and sunglasses and the groundsheet in case it should rain and the jungle oil in case it was a bad day for mosquitoes.

Outings—that lovely word for summery winds and quiet adventures when you lie on a blanket in the grass munching something delicious, reading *Robinson Crusoe,* gently scratching your mosquito bites—just the right distance from home.

THIRTEEN

THE week in July when it is always said to rain in Sweden brought a heat wave instead of rain. It started off hot, and on Sara's name day the temperature had gone up to 82 degrees Fahrenheit. On the following day it was 86, and there were threatening rumbles of thunder in the distance.

To start with, Sara and Gunilla really enjoyed the heat as they pedaled off on their bicycles to Goldfield Park, dressed in shorts and sun tops, but soon it became too much even for them.

That is, Gunilla never complained about the heat—she was used to much worse than this. Bosse had said that the temperature sometimes went up to 104–122 degrees in Persia in July.

However, the oppressive heat gave Sara a headache

and made her bad-tempered, and her back and arms were burned by the sun. At night they would sting and burn, and then the skin would peel off in great tender patches.

And although it was shady and pleasant under the trees in the park, it was even nicer in the garden at home with the garden hose and a box of ice cubes within reach. And even the most enthusiastic lover of outings can grow weary of drinking tepid fruit juice and eating hard-boiled eggs; also, in hot weather the horseflies around the old barn grew very active.

Still, it was all right for the girls because they could stay at home and take it easy. They could have showers and cold drinks and eat ice cream and lie on their backs in the grass under the trees, or they could take their clothes off and lie on their beds in a cool breeze. Things were worse for Mother and Father who had to be shut up in stuffy office buildings, working from nine until four in the afternoon, while the only "fresh air" that came in through the open windows consisted of gasoline fumes and the smell of melting asphalt.

"If we don't have a storm soon, I shall go crazy," Sara's mother gasped as she sat in a deck chair on the veranda one evening toward the end of the week. "The thunder is there, threatening all the time. If only it would break and clear the air . . ."

"Yes, what we need is some heavy rain that really gets down to the roots," Dad agreed as he stirred the cubes of ice in his glass. "It doesn't seem to help however much we water the garden—just look at those roses! And the lawn . . . just like the steppes! If it

104

keeps on like this, I'm sure we'll have our water rationed."

"Typical, isn't it, that it should be hot in July just because our holidays are in August this year," Mother continued, wiping a lank strand of hair from her forehead. "I wonder how the big children are getting on— we haven't heard from them for some time. Goodness, won't it be lovely to get to the real country soon!"

Sara was upstairs in bed, trying to sleep.

She was really very tired, and her head felt as heavy as a sandbag. But that comfortable sleepy feeling and those exciting waking dreams just wouldn't come.

Instead, her whole body seemed to be prickling with an unpleasant worried feeling, as though ants had gotten under her skin.

Although she was only wearing a short nightdress made of the thinnest cotton and had no blanket, only a sheet over her, she felt sticky and hot. She twisted and turned in the bed trying to find a spot that was still cool. Every time she turned over, the sheet seemed to twist itself up, too, and became a slinky damp snake clinging to her legs. The ribbons that she always tied her braids with at night had worked loose, so that her hair came around her neck and cheeks in a sticky, tickling mess. Her throat felt as dry, as it does when you have been asleep for a long time with your mouth open. But the water in the glass on her bedside table was tepid and stale.

It was not only the heat that troubled Sara, although it did make everything much worse.

The terrible thing was that she had quarreled with

Gunilla that afternoon. She lay there trying to remember how it had all happened.

Mother had said that she should try to be quite natural with Gunilla, just like with her other friends. And it certainly did happen now and then that she and Lena and Lasse and Anita had a fight and quarreled, but it was soon over, and nobody ever felt very bad about it afterward.

But things *weren't* the same with Gunilla. Not at all.

She really couldn't say how it had started. They were lying in the grass by the hedge cutting out paper dolls from a magazine. Sara chatted about this and that, as she usually did. Somehow she got to talking about their

106

cottage in the country, how lovely it was on dark eve-nings in August with a large red moon that would first lie there rocking like an orange boat above the trees and then grow larger and larger and become silvery white and cold, and how it made a wide glittering path of moonlight across the bay. And soon it would be the season for crayfish, and Dad had a brother in Småland who always used to send them lots—you know, those red crawling animals with claws that you cook with dill. . . . Well, that is, they are not red to start with—they are black, you see, and they are delicious and your hands get all sticky. And last year the whole family went out for a swim in the moonlight, and perhaps they'll do that this year as well when Bosse and Mar-gareta and Gunilla come out for a visit.

"That will be fun, won't it, Gunilla?"

". . . mmmmm . . ."

"Why don't you answer, Gunilla!"

"Moon . . . the moon . . ." Gunilla murmured.

"Well, what about it?" Sara asked rather impatiently. She thought that Gunilla ought to have agreed that it would be fun to visit them in the country and have crayfish and go bathing and boating. . . .

But Gunilla did not reply. She just lay on her back, staring up at the sky with her eyes open very wide.

"Can't you hear, Gunilla?" Sara felt a great wave of impatience rise up inside her. She grabbed hold of Gunilla's bare shoulder and shook her.

"*Say* something, Gunilla. Really, you're driving me mad!"

Suddenly all the tiredness and tension and worry and the effect of the heat seemed to boil up in Sara, and before she realized it, the words came pouring out, and she hit Gunilla's arm several times with her clenched fist.

"Why do you have to go around like that always saying nothing?" she screamed. She couldn't remember now where all the unkind words and reproaches came from. They were just there suddenly, pouring out like a waterfall, showering over Gunilla, who sat terror-stricken with her arms over her head, eyes black with fear.

Then all at once Gunilla leaned forward, lashing out with the quick movements of a cat, and hit Sara right on the mouth so hard that it began to bleed.

Sara was so surprised that she didn't even cry, although her lower lip was cut quite badly by her teeth and the blood was running down her fingers and staining her sun top.

When she raised her head again, Gunilla was gone.

She told Mum and Dad afterward that she had fallen and cut her mouth on a stone.

But what was going to happen tomorrow?

Could she just run across to Villa Valborg and tell Gunilla she was sorry? Was it . . . was it the sort of thing you could forgive . . . the sort of thing you could say, "Oh, that was nothing," about, and then start playing as usual?

If only she had been able to talk to Mother and Father! But they had looked so tired and worn when they got back from town that she never got around to it. What if Gunilla had told Bosse and Margareta that Sara had been nasty to her and had thumped her with her fists. Perhaps she would never be allowed to play there again.

And she had wanted to be kind and help Gunilla to become happy again . . . and *now* . . . the whole summer was spoiled, she felt. Tears welled up in her eyes and ran down her cheeks, making Sara's face feel even hotter and stickier. Her head began to throb again, and she had to put a corner of her pillow into her mouth to stop her sobs from being heard all over the house.

But soon the sobs came less frequently, and in some ways it was rather a relief to be crying. It made her feel light inside, although her head was heavy and thick.

A light evening breeze blew in through the window and caressed Sara's face like a cool hand. She drew in a deep sigh and felt as though the ants under her skin were settling down. "Tomorrow morning I can talk to Mother and Father about it," she thought vaguely, and all at once she was overcome by sleep.

109

FOURTEEN

"TOMORROW morning I can talk to Mother and Father" was the thought that Sara had comforted herself with before she went to sleep.

"Tomorrow morning" was all very well, but when Sara woke up from her deep sleep, it was half-past nine already, and Mum and Dad had left for work a long time ago.

On the bedside table there was a cup of tea in a Thermos and two sandwiches covered over with a plate, and a little note from Mother.

"Hi, Sara. We are off to town. We hadn't the heart to wake you, since you seemed to be sleeping so well. Look after yourself today and be careful on the road when you go shopping. The shopping list is on the kitchen table. Love from Mother and Dad!"

It was quite a little while before Sara remembered what had happened yesterday. But suddenly she caught sight of her sun top with bloodstains on it lying on the floor. *What was she to do?* Of course she couldn't just avoid going to Villa Valborg. In any case, she was supposed to be having lunch with them as usual.

She was undecided as she sat on the edge of her bed munching a cheese sandwich and drinking warm tea. Her hair was untidy, and her face was puffy from sleep and pale under the freckles.

Undecided, she went to the bathroom and washed her face and cleaned her teeth. Her lip was swollen and sore. Undecided, she braided her hair, put on a pair of clean shorts, and pulled the bedspread up over a very rough and ready attempt at making the bed.

Undecided, she went downstairs and out onto the veranda. The air was as hot and still as it had been for the last few days, and the sky was covered with dark bluish clouds.

"I'll go shopping now, first thing," she thought, feeling suddenly energetic, and ran back indoors to get the shopping list and her sandals.

She was standing by the kitchen table in front of the open window when she heard Margareta calling. Their kitchen window looked out onto the hedge. It was impossible to see what was going on in the next door garden, but you could hear quite clearly if anyone called.

Sara raised her head and listened.

"Gunilla, Gunilla, come back—*Gunilla*, can't you hear me? Come back!"

Sara dropped the bag with her purse and the shopping list and rushed to the door.

"Gunilla . . ."

A moment later Sara was by the hedge. She slipped through the hole and into the garden next door.

"What's the matter, Margareta?" she called, rushing up to the veranda where Margareta stood, looking very pale and leaning against one of the posts.

"Have you seen Gunilla? Where did she go? She took her bicycle and rushed off."

"I didn't see her," Sara said. "I was in the kitchen and heard nothing until you called."

"Oh, you must help me, Sara! Bosse is away. He went to Malmö on the night train, and you see . . . I . . . have hurt my foot. I fell on the stairs as I was going to run after Gunilla. Oh, what shall I do? I can't cycle after her with this foot—it just won't carry me." She tried to put her weight on the foot, but raised it again, screwing her face up with pain.

"I'll get my bike and go after her," Sara said eagerly, and started toward the gate. "Don't worry, Margareta. I think I know where she is . . . but . . ." She stopped suddenly and went very red. "Why did she go off like that? Had anything special happened?"

"Yes, Sara, I was very hasty . . . I completely lost my temper. You see, I slept so badly last night because of the heat and because Gunilla was so strange in the evening. She cried in her sleep and tossed about—but we'll talk about that later, Sara. Just hurry off and try to find her before she gets too far . . . and before the thunderstorm breaks. I just heard some rumbling, and they said in the weather forecast that . . ."

But Sara was gone.

112

Her bicycle stood conveniently ready by the garden gate. It was not meant to be left there. Mother and Father kept telling her to put it away in the garage at night, but it seemed impossible for her to remember. For once her carelessness came in very handy. She did not bother to go indoors to get her sandals—she just flung herself onto the bicycle and shot off down the dusty road.

"She must have gone off to Goldfield Park," Sara thought. "That's the only place where you can hide around here. She can't have gone up to the main road —there's so much traffic, and a policeman by the crossroads. Oh dear, poor Margareta! What if her foot was broken? And poor, poor Gunilla. She might crash and hurt herself. She wasn't very good at cycling yet . . ."

Sara stopped for a moment when she got to the open area called Goldfield Park. The clouds were hanging like huge gray feather bolsters over the fields, and the tall trees stood there with drooping leaves as if waiting for something to happen. The birds twittered anxiously, and the swallows that lived under the eaves of the barn roof were flying very close to the ground.

"She is sure to be in the barn," thought Sara as she struggled up the winding road that led to the derelict building. Mud that had dried as hard as stone formed rough, bumpy ridges on the road, and the bicycle rattled and shook. Sara's feet smarted, and her chest ached.

She dropped the bicycle in the grass by the entrance to the barn and rushed in. The barn was empty, apart

from an ancient threshing machine in a corner and a few dejected bales of dusty broken-down hay along one of the walls. The loft above was quite empty and very rough and dilapidated, with broken floorboards and occasional large holes. The ladder that once led up to the loft had long since disappeared, and it was almost impossible to get up there unless you were as agile as a monkey. Sara had never dreamed of climbing up there, but she remembered that one of her brothers or sisters had told her that Annika once got up there with tremendous difficulty and then she nearly fell through the rotten floor and broke her neck. Sven had stood below, telling her off for being so foolish.

"Gunilla—are you there? Gunilla, hey, hey! *Gunilla, where are you?!*"

No reply—that was strange. Sara had felt so sure that Gunilla would be in the barn. There were not many other good hiding places around here . . . but wait a moment . . .

Sara had been rooting around in the hay, just to make sure. Now she stopped. Could Gunilla have gone down to the old air-raid shelter on the hill a little closer to town? She certainly was not in the barn.

Sara walked around the old threshing machine to make sure that even a slim little girl could not be hiding behind it. But what about the bicycle? If Gunilla was in the barn, her bicycle should have been lying outside.

Where on earth could she be?

Dejected, Sara went out and got on her bike. A heavy drop of rain fell on her bare back as she leaned forward over the handlebars. She looked up at the sky. Thunderclouds hung there like a threatening blue-black canopy or an enormous stomach full of stones. The distant rumbling that she had thought was the traffic on the main road suddenly seemed to come roaring over her head . . .

Oh, goodness! Sara felt a sudden quick stab of terror go through her. Not that she was really frightened of thunder—at least, not at home, with a grownup.

But here, in the middle of a field, it was different.

A tiny white figure against a dark background . . . a good target for the thunder-man to aim at . . . bang, bang!

Should she turn back? She remembered Gunilla and pedaled on as the rain fell harder and harder. The wind blew in great sudden gusts shaking the treetops and flattening the long grass against the ground like well-brushed hair.

She had forgotten that it was so far to the old shelter. Her hair and back were soaking wet already, and although she bent her head forward as far as she could, the rain whipped her face and made her cheeks sting. There, at last!

She left her bicycle on the ground and made her way through the thick undergrowth that concealed the entrance.

It was locked. An enormous padlock was on a thick iron door!

Oh, *no!*

Nothing to do except turn back. But *where* could

Gunilla be? Sara stood there helpless, on the verge of tears, staring at the unfriendly door. Where on earth . . .

At that moment the first clap of thunder came.

A sudden primitive fear made Sara throw herself onto the bicycle again and rush back the way she had come. The dry, bumpy road had turned into a bumpy river, with water swirling around the pedals of the bicycle. An enormous white flash of lightning flared up behind the gray outline of the water tower. Sara counted desperately, "One, two, thr . . ." Crash!

"O-o-o-o-o-o!" Sara moaned, and for a moment she forgot everything in the world except her own fear and her intense wish to escape from this rumbling, flashing, pouring iron sky that looked as though it might fall down any moment and crush her.

The rotten wooden frame of the barn creaked and whistled, and the rain poured in through the broken roof, making great puddles on the stone floor. But to Sara it seemed like home as she dragged herself in on shaking legs and flung herself in a corner on a pile of dirty hay.

The hay was prickly and sharp against her bare skin, but she did not feel it. Neither did she notice the sores on her feet or the scratches on her arms.

She lay on her back with her eyes shut listening to her own violent breathing. Once again the sky flared up. One . . . two . . . crash, bang, bang.

FIFTEEN

FOR about fifteen minutes the center of the thunderstorm remained over the park and Sara's head.

Flashes of lightning came one after the other like white flames, and Sara never counted more than *one* before the crash of thunder followed the flash. The rain was like a thick, steaming sheet or curtain outside the entrance to the barn.

Sara lay in the same position with her eyes tightly closed. But even so, she saw the flashes of lightning. She lay quite still so as not to attract the attention of the thunder god. If she did not move, perhaps he would not notice her or bother to throw lightning at the barn.

Of course she knew perfectly well that it was not a question of a thunder god riding around in the sky but something to do with electricity and clouds that bumped into each other. But just at the moment she couldn't think very clearly. Lightning—thunder . . . lightning—thunder . . . was it *never* going to stop? And then, with surprising suddenness, it was all over!

It was so sudden that Sara hardly grasped what had happened. She still kept counting, but now . . . one . . . two . . . three . . . four . . . five. . . . The rain was different, too, as though the thunder god had pulled up the curtain of rain and just made do with a little ordinary summer rain . . . drip . . . drip . . .

Soon even the dripping stopped, and everything was surprisingly silent. Sara sat up and noticed that she was shivering with cold.

She looked around rather cautiously and tried to warm her cold shoulders with her arms. It was as though she had awakened from a noisy nightmare.

Then she heard someone speaking.

She looked toward the door. Perhaps somebody had come to look for her? No, all she could see was gray mist, wet grass, dripping trees. Her eyes wandered around the barn, searching. Then she heard the voice again, louder this time. Where . . . *where?*

She stared up toward the roof—it was coming from *above.* . . . Surely nobody was up there? How strange it was . . . odd foreign sounds. Now they were getting louder—shrill cries!

She wanted to call out, "Is anyone there?" But she could only produce a croak. She tried again, but the result was a pathetic whisper.

The stranger up there under the roof went on talking

and talking and screaming. It truly was a foreign language.

Now Sara recognized the voice—it was *Gunilla,* and she was speaking Persian! Suddenly Sara's stiff body came to life. She rushed over to the opening of the loft where the ladder had once been and shouted, and this time her voice was heard.

"Gunilla!" she shouted as loud as she could. "Gunilla, are you there? Gunilla, please answer me!"

The voice just continued screaming and sobbing.

Sara looked around helplessly. How had Gunilla managed to get up there? Could she really have climbed up on the slanted beam by the end wall of the barn?

Sara remembered vaguely that that was where her sister Annika was supposed to have climbed up. There was a hole in the floor of the loft just by the wall where the beam passed it and continued up toward the roof. If you got that far, you could squeeze through the hole, but . . . but . . .

Sara shuddered. "Gunilla!" she called again, on the verge of tears. "Answer, please, *please* answer! What are you doing up there? Gunilla!"

To her relief she heard a shuffling noise, and a moment later Gunilla's face appeared by the edge of the large hole just above Sara's head. She was dirty, and her hair was straggly and untidy. She was lying on her stomach and seemed to be staring straight down at Sara, but Sara got the odd feeling that Gunilla didn't really see her.

Silent and trembling, Sara stood there waiting, her heart thumping violently.

121

Then the voice started again, the strange, shrill foreign voice. But now it was speaking Swedish.

". . . I'm running and running . . . but I can still hear it, although it's farther away. . . . She is calling my name. . . . 'Come back,' she says, 'come back, Mahnaz, and I'll give you a whipping!' But I didn't hit him hard, although it did bleed. I ran away and hid under the bushes, and my chest hurts terribly, but I can't hear Mother's voice any more. . . . Miss Brown says that God punishes you if you are disobedient. . . . Asgar's nose was bleeding . . . and suddenly the earth trembled and trembled and shook and then the roar, the tremendous roar, and the earth broke open. 'Oh . . . come,' she called, 'Mahnaz, come back. . . .' "

The sound of the voice turned into a screaming sob.

"Gunilla," Sara whispered, horrified. "Don't be unhappy, please, Gunilla. It's all right, Gunilla."

But Gunilla did not hear her. She was talking to herself or to some invisible person far away. Sometimes she spoke Swedish, sometimes Persian; sometimes her voice was clear and shrill; sometimes it was half muffled by sobs.

". . . it was so very, very dark, and I stumbled on and on, and I was screaming because I couldn't find my way back, and all around me these terrible noises, dust and gravel and stones everywhere, and I dug and dug with my hands, and there she was under the beam from the roof and Granny and Asgar. . . . It was my fault, all my fault. . . . The missionaries said

122

that if you have sinned, you must be punished, and if I hadn't run away from Mother, the earth wouldn't have opened with a terrible roar and made the roof fall down."

The jerky, distracted words came down from the loft like a dreadful lament to Sara, gazing up with a face that was pale and tense.

" 'Come back and I'll give you a whipping, Mahnaz . . . come back . . .' "

At the beginning, Sara thought Gunilla was talking about how she ran away from Margareta, but suddenly she realized the truth. Her dismay was mixed with excitement, almost joy.

It had happened. The thing they had all been waiting for had happened. Something had made Gunilla remember. Mahnaz—*Mahnaz*—that must be her name —*her real name*.

"Asgar took my meat—my lovely big piece of meat —and he only left me the rice. . . . Mother made a lovely kebab, and it smelled delicious . . . and Asgar took mine. . . . I didn't hit him hard . . . but he was younger, and Granny and Mother sometimes liked him best, and Granny told Mother, and Mother's eyes were angry . . ."

Her sobs grew louder, and she slid nearer the hole in the floor. Sara forgot everything except her fear that Gunilla would fall down.

"Oh, if only a grownup would come," she moaned to herself. But who? Margareta could not come because of her foot . . . and Bosse was away . . . and

123

nobody would be walking about the park in a thunder-storm.

So there was only Sara. But what could *she* do?

She glanced quickly up at the wall and the beam where Gunilla must have climbed up. Would she dare to do it herself? The thought made Sara even colder than she was before. She was so bad at gym, and heights made her feel dizzy.

" 'Come back . . . come back . . .' but I ran past the neighbors' house and past the wall and I hid among the bushes, and the sky was completely black without any stars, and I lay there for a long, long time, although I felt cold."

"Be careful, Gunilla! You might fall down."

". . . those who disobey their father and mother will suffer punishment . . . and the poplars rustled and rustled and I . . . can't remember . . . can't remember. . . . There was gravel on their eyes and pieces of Grandfather's water pipe . . . and strange people came, and I screamed and screamed, and they all asked and asked what's your name . . . what is your name . . . what is your name?"

The voice up there became a whisper, and although Sara stood on tiptoe listening and hardly daring to breathe, she could no longer hear the words. Gunilla's head slowly sank down toward the edge of the opening; she seemed completely exhausted and about to go to sleep or faint.

"What if she faints and falls down," Sara thought in a panic. "Gunilla," she shouted again, as loud as she could. "Gunilla, be careful! You might fall down. Can

124

you hear me? It is Sara. Can't you see me, Gunilla, here right below you on the floor?"

But Gunilla did not reply. She just rolled over onto one side. One more slight movement and she would fall straight through the hole.

Desperate, Sara rushed over to the end wall of the barn where Gunilla had climbed up. She gazed upward. . . . Oh, God, she would never manage it . . . but she must be quick.

Cautiously she put one foot on the jutting edge of the beam, leaned forward, and tried to get hold of the wall with her hand. There was a nail, but it was sharp and rusty, and it slipped out of her hand as she tried to pull herself up and get her other foot onto the beam as well. If only she wasn't trembling so!

At last she was standing upright with both her feet on the beam. Now the thing was to take a step, to bring one foot forward and upward without losing her balance. Carefully, carefully, oh, she could *never* do it!

Gasping, she leaned against the wall, her throat full of sobs. Then she raised her head and caught sight of a piece of rope hanging just above her head. Gunilla must have used that when she climbed up there. But before she could reach it, she had to take several steps —oh, help, help, now she's moaning up there. Perhaps she'll move, shift her body, and fall. . . . Sara supported herself against the wall and lifted her foot, then another step . . . and another. . . . One more step and she would be able to reach out her hand for the rope.

"Sara! Gunilla! Are you there?"

Sara flung herself to the floor. Then she limped to the entrance.

"Daddy, Daddy, she'll fall down, she'll fall down!" Sara screamed, and then burst into tears, sobbing violently.

SIXTEEN

MANY hours later as Sara lay in her bed with Teddy on her arm and the old blue cardigan under her cheek and a large glass of fruit juice by the bed, it all seemed like a strange dream.

There she lay, and everything was just the same as usual. But her feet were bandaged, and she had a damp cloth on her forehead.

The evening sun shone in through the window and was reflected in the glass of red fruit juice. Ulrika sat in the basket chair staring in front of her; there was an old comic in the dust under the chest of drawers and a half-eaten sandwich on the edge of the table. Three flies buzzed about the ceiling, and in the corner hung a daddy longlegs.

There was a pleasant smell of cooking from the

kitchen mixed with the smell of roses from the garden and a whiff of disinfectant from her feet.

The cat Laban was curled up asleep on Sara's old underpants on the chair.

Downstairs in the sitting room Mother sat at the piano, playing very softly.

> "The birds are all sleeping
> Wings over head.
> The fishes are keeping
> In their reed bed.
> The moon riding high
> Shines alone in the sky.
> Foxes and reindeer
> Lie under the wood—
> Lullaby now, dear,
> Lose your dark mood.
> Everything seems
> Summertime in your dreams!"

Sara joined in and hummed the old familiar lullaby that Mother had sung to all of them and that usually made them as sleepy as kittens. The idea was that Sara should go to sleep. She had had a bath and a hot drink and a pill that the doctor had given her. Her body felt warm and heavy and seemed to be drifting off to sleep.

But her head would not be soothed. All the little sleeping birds in the world could not stop her restless thoughts running around like mice under the damp cloth on her forehead.

She was a little scared of going to sleep. She was

afraid that she would not be able to get away from all the horrors . . . that the horrors would go on and on.

Mother sang:

> "Patches of sunlight
> Play on the wall,
> Sleep, little one, shut your eyes
> To the world . . ."

But Sara felt sure that frightening memories would come back in her dreams. It was better to stay awake and think about things. Anyway, she did not want to be asleep when Dad came back from the hospital and told them how Gunilla was. Margareta was going to stay with her, and Mother had telephoned Bosse in Malmö and told him what had happened. He would be coming back on the night train.

Again and again Sara's thoughts returned, in spite of herself, to the events in the barn. They went back to the awful minutes when she stood there alone, waiting, while Dad went off to fetch a ladder from one of the houses nearby. It had seemed like a hundred years!

Before Dad rushed off, he had dragged out a large armful of hay and put it under the hole, but the hay was old and limp, so if anything had happened, it probably would not have been much use.

Sara had stood very quietly so as not to rouse Gunilla. She stayed there with her arms stretched out, staring up at the hole where Gunilla's motionless form could just be glimpsed. Every now and then a soft moan could be heard from up there, and Sara held her breath with terror.

"I shall never forget it in all my life," she thought, holding Teddy and the cardigan closer. "Never, never . . ."

And yet, in the midst of all the terror a hopeful thought had occurred to her. No, probably it was not then, for at that moment when she just stood there waiting and waiting, shivering with cold and with teeth chattering and her head throbbing—all she felt was fear, just a terrible fear.

In actual fact the "hundred years" probably lasted only about five minutes. Dad had not only managed to find a long ladder, but he also found the owner of the ladder, a kind old man who was in his garden look-ing at the damage done to his roses by the rain. He came along and helped Dad to get Gunilla down from the loft and carry her to their car up by the main road. In the car Margareta sat waiting; poor Margareta with her sprained foot was frantic with anxiety over what might have happened to Gunilla and Sara in the storm.

Then they had all driven off to the hospital . . . and Gunilla had awakened in the car and mumbled something in Persian . . . and Margareta had looked at Sara questioningly, and Sara had nodded and said, "Yes, I think it has happened at last. . . ."

After that they had been taken in charge by a friendly nurse and a kind young doctor, and Sara had told them about everything. Then another doctor came along with an older man whom they called Professor, and they had looked at Gunilla and put her on a stretcher. Margareta sat in a wheelchair after the first doctor had seen to her foot—and Dad had telephoned for Mother to come, and the nurse had washed and bandaged Sara's feet and put a bandage on her knee that she had scratched when she jumped down off the beam. Then Dad wrapped Sara in a rug from the car, and Mother took her home while Dad stayed on.

"Patches of sunlight
Play on the wall . . ."

Mother sang, and Sara murmured the last line of the lullaby as she snuggled down into her pillow. The nice "forgetting pill" the doctor had given her had begun to work, and soon Sara drifted gently off into a deep, dreamless slumber.

131

She slept so deeply that she did not hear Dad come back and put the car in the garage, nor did she hear Mum and Dad talking to each other quietly, or know that the house was filled with the smell of coffee and the clatter of cups and the noise of the telephone ringing.

She slept so deeply that she did not even notice that Mum and Dad came in and carried her bed into their room and put it by the foot of their bed, just as they used to when Sara had mumps or whooping cough years ago.

When she slept in their room, the good thing was that if she woke up in the night feeling worried, she only had to step across and snuggle down under the blankets with them.

However, Sara did not wake up from her sleep this particular night. Only when the alarm clock went off at seven the following morning did she open her eyes and look around. Slowly it dawned on her that it was the lamp in her parents' bedroom that was hanging above her bed.

"Oh," she exclaimed gaily, and sat up in bed with a jerk. "Am I ill?"

Then she remembered. "Oh, Dad, what did they say about Gunilla at the hospital?"

"Not much as yet," Dad replied. "She will have to stay there for observation, as they call it. But I think that the doctor was very hopeful about her.

"Of course, she was completely exhausted, but even so, there was something useful and healthy about this outburst. The doctor told Margareta that Gunilla has been imagining that somehow it was her fault that the earthquake occurred. Then when she was taken in by the missionaries and they kept talking about sin and punishments, she felt even more certain that she had caused the disaster by being disobedient."

"Oh, I understand," Sara exclaimed. "She heard her mother calling and calling, and she didn't reply. And that is why she wanted to try and forget the name completely. *Mahnaz*—it's a pretty name, I think. I wonder if she will want to use that now instead of Gunilla?"

"It is said to mean 'The Moonlike One,' Margareta told me," Dad added.

"Moonlike? Oh, then that was why Gunilla looked strange when I talked about the moonlight in the country. But, Dad, how long do you think she will have to stay in the hospital?"

"At least a week, Margareta thought."

"A week! Then we will have moved to the country before she gets home," Sara said unhappily. "What an awful shame!"

"Perhaps you will be able to visit her in the hospital," Mother suggested. "And I was thinking, perhaps we might ask if Gunilla could come and stay with us for a while when she is better. What do you say to that idea?"

"Super, Mother, absolutely super! What fun that would be!" Sara flung her arms around her Mother's neck and gave her a good hug. "But . . ." Sara had a sudden thought. "But perhaps Gunilla won't want to leave Margareta and Bosse."

133

"Perhaps all three of them could come, then," Mother replied. "I am sure they can stop working on the house for a week, at least. They could sleep in the chalet."

SEVENTEEN

THE day after the thunderstorm was a quiet one—a real "day-after" day.

Fortunately Mother could stay at home, and she and Sara had a peaceful, cool, drizzly time together. The temperature had dropped more than ten degrees, and the air that came in through the open windows seemed almost chilly. From the garden came a pleasant smell of damp earth and newly washed flowers, and the grass seemed to have grown greener overnight. Sara sat by the kitchen table, and for the first time in weeks she was wearing a sweater. She felt a little strange, not ill exactly, but washed-out and weary—tired and a bit dizzy and excited at the same time. Her face was pale underneath the suntan, and that made her look a little green, and her eyelids were heavy and swollen after her heavy sleep.

When you feel like that, it is very pleasant just to potter around peacefully at home with Mother or Father, doing nothing in particular . . . play a little with a doll perhaps, and do a bit of sewing on her new bathrobe . . . read some old book that has been read many times before . . . play the piano a bit . . . not have a proper lunch, just nibble at fruit and drink lemonade . . . play a record, sleep a little, talk a lot with Mother, or just sit next to her looking at nothing in particular.

There were many pleasant things to talk about on a day like this when Sara needed something to soothe her mind.

For instance, they talked about the new dinghy that Dad had bought after the old one sprang a leak and sank. It was going to have a mast and a sail—a square red sail—and Sara had made a little three-cornered flag for the top of the mast with *Augusta* embroidered on it in red.

They also talked about Sara's new room in the attic of their summer cottage. Up to now Sara had always slept in the same room as Mother and Father, but last spring they had had a room made for Sara in the attic —a room that she would have all to herself. A local carpenter had put up walls and boxed in the attic window with plywood and made a built-in double bunk. There was a proper door with a lock and a ceiling light and a bedside lamp so that you could read in bed without having to hold a flashlight in your hand. Now that they were going there for a holiday, the room was going

136

to be papered and painted and furnished. Dad had already bought the paint, and Mother had found some leftover rolls of their bedroom wallpaper with blue flowers.

At the moment, Mother and Sara were discussing the question of curtains.

Mother had looked through her box of remnants and found several pieces of curtain material that would do for the little attic window. Should they choose white curtains with little red squares on them or plain white with drawnwork or pale blue with pink rosebuds?

And should they just have a frill at the top or panels at the sides or both? And should they hang straight down or be tied at the sides with bows? These were nice problems to discuss.

Sara finally settled for the blue curtains with rosebuds, and they would be tied with ribbon the same color as the roses. "Oh, it does sound beautiful, Mother," Sara exclaimed. "Terrific, in fact."

"And you can have the old blue bedspreads that used to be in the nursery. They are rather faded, but still quite good. I'll dig them out so that we can have them washed before we go."

"Do you think the room will be done by the time Gunilla comes out there?" Sara asked excitedly. "Then we can live up there together."

"That depends on how long she will have to stay in the hospital," Mother replied. "Perhaps Bosse will have some news for us this afternoon."

And so their thoughts were back with Gunilla again.

Sara dropped the piece of curtain she had been holding and sat silent. Mother's presence, the smell of the sponge cake cooking in the oven, the chatter about colors and rosebuds and frills all seemed to fade, and other images came into her mind. Now it was not so much the things that had happened in the barn yesterday that occupied her thoughts. As it had all ended well and Gunilla was unhurt, she could forget that.

But now she could not help thinking about what Gunilla had said . . . the whole story of what had happened during the earthquake. It was only afterward that Gunilla's words had sunk in, and now she could not forget them.

Sara had been waiting and longing for the secret to be cleared up, for the door of the dark cave to be unlocked so that the princess could get out, liberated and happy, and talk and talk. Now the door was wide open, suddenly, and things were not so simple.

Sara's dreams about how she had gone out to the strange country like a brave knight searching for the lost name and the key to the heart of the princess—these had been exciting fairy tales.

Now she no longer needed to dream those dreams. Now when she lay on her bed or sat silent at the kitchen table or in the rocking chair, no fairy tales came to her.

What she heard instead was a true story told in Gunilla's own voice, and it was terrible and full of tears and death, and when she thought of it, Sara wanted to put her arms around Mother and stay close to her warmth and comfort.

At the same time she realized that it was a good thing for Gunilla to be able to talk about all that. When she could talk about it, it would lose its power.

"I ought to be happy, Mother," she whispered, "so why do I feel as though I only want to cry?"

"Darling," Mother said, and put down her sewing. She took Sara on her lap as she used to long ago. "You cry as much as you like. It will do you good to cry, just as it did Gunilla good to talk. You have had a difficult experience, too. So, of course, it will have an effect —it's not surprising at all."

Sara put her head on Mother's shoulder and cried until Mother's blouse was quite wet with her tears, and

139

there they sat until the smell from the oven told them that the cake must be done.

Just as they had turned the cake out of the tin to cool and put the kettle on for tea, they heard footsteps outside on the veranda.

"Hello, is anyone in?" It was Bosse's voice. "We are home again, Margareta and I," he said as he came into the kitchen, "and we were wondering if you would like to come over for a chat. Margareta is going back to the hospital; she only came home to fetch some clothes. The Professor has arranged for her to stay with Gunilla for the next few days, but she would very much like to see you, and we're just making some coffee."

"And, as you see, we have made a cake!"

Margareta was sitting on a sofa with her foot up on a cushion. She looked happy, although she was pale and tired. It almost seemed to Sara as though she had a new face—it had a sort of radiance about it. Bosse looked young and happy, too, as if he were the same age as one of Sara's brothers rather than a solid engineer of thirty-six.

"I can't believe it's true," Margareta said, smiling. "It is just like a miracle, much more exciting than a story out of *A Thousand and One Nights*. I feel so happy now, and to think how desperate I was yesterday when I thought I had lost her forever because of my outburst."

Sara suddenly went red. She remembered that she had not told them why Gunilla had behaved so strangely the night before.

"Oh, Margareta . . . Bosse . . . you don't know
. . ." she stammered. "It was all . . . it was all my
fault . . . you see. I . . . the thing was . . . it was
so hot, and I got terribly cross with her, and I punched
her with my fists, and then she hit me on my mouth, and
it started to bleed—" Sara stopped in mid-sentence and
stood there with her mouth open; then she went on.
"Just like she did with her little brother that evening.
And then she ran away . . . and I was scared . . . I
didn't know what . . . I didn't dare tell anybody!"

Sara's tears had been very close, and now they began
to flow.

"Come, come, little Sara, don't cry," Bosse said
quickly. "It's nothing to be unhappy about. On the contrary, it was a good thing, the doctor said, that something happened to bring the whole thing to a head. For
such a long time she had borne this terrible burden all
by herself, poor little thing—the idea that she had
caused the earthquake by being disobedient! And all of
us being so kind and understanding just made her
guilty conscience worse, the doctor said. So, in fact,
you did her a very great service, Sara!"

Sara smiled and wiped her tears on her sleeve.

"You see, it was a whole train of events that brought
the matter to a head," Margareta continued. "It started
the evening before, then I lost my temper, and after that
there was the thunderstorm."

"Now I understand," Sara said thoughtfully. "I understand *exactly*. When the thunderstorm came and it
began rumbling, Gunilla thought that it was another

141

earthquake because she had run away from Margareta, and Margareta called and called her name just as her mother had done that evening of the earthquake . . ."

"Yes, all the past that had been hidden away inside her came to the surface, and she heard the name . . . her real name—Mahnaz, Mahnaz, and she could talk about it up there in the loft. It all came bursting out and liberated her," Bosse said with a smile.

"But of course everything is not over yet," Margareta added. "The doctor wants her to stay in the hospital for some weeks so that they can examine her thoroughly and talk to her so that she gradually will get rid of her terrible memories. Of course she will never forget completely, but the important thing is that she can think about her memories without having any strange guilt feelings about what happened."

"Oh, yes," Sara agreed sensibly as she took a large bite of the warm sponge cake. "To be unhappy is nasty, but to have a guilty conscience is really awful! But what shall we call her when she gets back?" she continued eagerly. "Will she want us to go on calling her Gunilla, or will she want to be called Mahnaz?"

"She said this morning that she wants to keep the name Gunilla to show that she really is Swedish," Margareta told them. "But she would like to have Mahnaz as her second name!"

"Then she'll have three names! Gunilla Mary Mahnaz—that sounds lovely! Oh dear, why do I have only the name Sara? Couldn't I have a few extra special names like Ursula or Elinor or Barbara or something?"

142

"Your name is Sara Clara." Mother laughed. "That will have to do! Now we really must go home and put the potatoes on. And later this week we must discuss if and when you can come and see us in the country."

"Oh yes, we must!" Sara shouted, jumping up and down.

EIGHTEEN

"AAAH, this is the life!" Sara's dad exclaimed, stepping out onto the rickety landing stage in his faded old shorts. He looked down lovingly at the new dinghy *Augusta* rubbing gently against the old tires that he had hung out so that his beautiful boat would not be scratched when he sailed into the harbor.

"Yes, this is heaven." Mother sighed, turning over to expose her pale side to the sun. Her eyes wandered happily up to the cottage with sunlight glittering on the open windows and a blaze of nasturtiums around the porch.

"It's super—super—super," Sara shouted from her rubber dinghy, bobbing up and down gently on the water. She paddled slowly with her hands on the sides of the dinghy as she lay on her stomach gazing into the water. Sometimes it was dark blue and sinister, sometimes sparkling green with glimpses of a sandy bottom and slippery underwater plants.

"Miauuu," Laban said as he lay on the roof of the shed lazily watching a bird.

It was the first day of their holiday, and the weather was perfect, not a cloud in the sky and a light southerly breeze fluttering the rushes and filling the red sails of Dad's dinghy.

Everything around them seemed to be just right: the gently lapping waves, the fragrant smell of clover, the tapping of the woodpecker, the cuckoo calling in the distance, and the sea gulls swooping overhead.

Sara on her rocking rubber dinghy could still feel in her mouth the tiny pips from the first ripe wild strawberries of the summer that she had found in the sheltered patch behind the woodshed.

Soon she would walk through the forest with a tin can to see how far the bilberries had gotten and to see if the hut from last year was still there in the clearing where the woodcutters worked.

Soon they would have their first sail to the barren islands out by the lighthouse with coffee in a Thermos and pancakes to eat.

Soon Sara and Mother would sit and scrape new potatoes and watch Dad cleaning herrings while the sea gulls screeched overhead.

"I don't think we should ever let the cottage again," Sara murmured, lifting her head.

"Never again," Mother replied, turning over on the

rocks. "Next summer I shall take time off from my job," she continued, picking an ant off her arm.

"Super!" Sara exclaimed, although she remembered that Mother said this every year. But even so it did sound good.

The dinghy rocked, and the sun beat down, and, after all, a month is a month.

How wonderful to show all this to Gunilla!

She had never roamed about in a forest with pine needles and moss underfoot and squirrels chattering in the treetops, or splashed about in a shallow warm bay, or grilled sausages among the stones out on the headland.

Think of all the people who didn't have holidays like this. Before this summer Sara had never thought of such things. She had somehow taken life for granted as it was.

"Don't go to sleep, Sara Clara. You might drift out to sea and never come back," Mother called to her, sitting up.

"I'm not asleep, I'm thinking," Sara replied, opening her eyes to watch a gull diving for a fish. "I'm thinking about the world . . ."

"We'll have to hurry up and get your room in the attic finished so that Gunilla can live up there with you when they come," Mother replied, realizing what made Sara think about the "world."

"I wonder if she has changed now . . . now, after what happened," Sara said after a while, feeling a little twinge of anxiety. "Perhaps she is quite a different girl now."

"More cheerful, I'm sure, and easier to talk to," Mother reassured her.

This proved to be quite true.

When Bosse and Margareta and Gunilla arrived at the cottage a few weeks later, Sara went to meet them, her heart thumping with excitement. She suddenly felt as shy as if she were meeting a completely strange girl.

"Hello, Gunilla!"

"Hello, Sara!"

They shook hands in awkward embarrassment, the way people do. Gunilla was a little pale, but her face shone with pleasure as she looked at Sara. Sara giggled a little and hung her head.

"I have a red rubber dinghy with me," Gunilla said, dropping a plastic-covered roll in front of Sara's feet.

"Great, I have a blue one," Sara exclaimed, looking up with a big grin.

"And a duck and a fish and a box of chocolates for you," Gunilla said, looking even happier. "And water wings for me as I can't swim yet."

"Super!" Sara shouted, jumping up and down.

When Sara had grown calmer and she and Gunilla were walking arm in arm down the narrow path to the cottage, she looked more closely at Gunilla's face to see if she had changed. And she noticed that there was something different about her, although it was hard to say what it could be. Perhaps it was something about the eyes—they no longer seemed to be on their guard; they had no secret to conceal.

A little later the girls were upstairs in Sara's new

room in the attic, unpacking Gunilla's things. The grownups drinking coffee below could hear their chatter bubbling and flowing like a stream. And soon after that happy shouts could be heard from the bathing beach.

Of course it was a wonderful week, the week when Sara showed Gunilla her summer paradise. The weather god smiled on them and made the sun shine and the bilberries ripen.

The wind blew from the east and was just right for driving *Augusta* this way and that among green islands and gray skerries and for chasing bluebottles and horseflies inland to the farmer's fields where they belonged.

Sara and Gunilla bathed and romped and splashed in the water and dozed on their rubber dinghies. They built huts, picked berries, and made toffee, and they came home with large bunches of wild flowers and the first mushrooms tied up in a handkerchief. But above all they talked. They talked about everything between heaven and earth, but more than anything else about school.

The thing was that Gunilla was going to be in Sara's class at school in the autumn—what fun that would be! Margareta and Bosse had been to see the headmaster of Sara's school before they left town, and he had promised to put Gunilla in the same section as Sara so that Sara could help her to settle down. Sara had shouted for joy when she heard the news.

In the evenings Sara would lie in bed telling Gunilla

all about the children at school and the teachers and the helpers in the dining room and the school nurse and the caretaker and basketball and all the games they played and the skating rink and the swings and the bicycle stands.

Soon Gunilla knew *everything*. She knew that the homeroom teacher was called Andy Pandy and the singing teacher Squeaky Dora. She knew that the caretaker was OK but rather strict . . . that the school nurse was sweet and the helpers in the dining room all grumpy save one . . . that Anders was the best in the class at all subjects, but Kristian was best in singing and gym . . . that Ove was a telltale and Bibbi boasted about her father's lovely car . . . but most of them were nice, especially Susanna and Johanna, who were twins and so alike that even the teachers couldn't tell them apart.

But a week is not very long, and soon it was the day before the morning when Margareta and Bosse and Gunilla were going back to town. Although it was not going to be very long before Sara and her parents went back, too, it was sad all the same.

To make the parting a little easier for them, the weather god hid the sun behind the clouds and sent off a hard, chilly west wind that lashed up white horses on the bay and made Mother close windows and look for sweaters.

"You can tell autumn is nearly here," she said. "The birch trees out on the headland are turning yellow already."

Night fell as black as ink, and Gunilla and Sara lay in their beds listening to the wind whining in the pine trees. They lay gazing out of the little attic window, but no stars were visible.

"Soon it will be Christmas," Sara exclaimed suddenly, pulling the bedclothes up to her chin. "That is great fun, you know. Oh yes, you had Christmas with the missionaries—what did you do? Was it fun?"

"Well," said Gunilla, "I suppose it was. We sang hymns and things and wore our Sunday dresses, and ladies with elegant hats came and gave us a parcel each . . . books of poetry and toys that one is too old to play with and so on. And then we had turkey for dinner, I think . . ."

150

"Turkey!" Sara exclaimed. *"Turkey!* Didn't you have ham and sausages and brawn and applesauce and liver paté and . . . ?"

Then Sara told Gunilla about their own Christmas from the evening two days before Christmas Eve when everybody settles down to write verses on the parcels and drink hot punch to the solemn moment after Christmas dinner when Mother goes to the piano and plays all the familiar carols.

She described how you cut frills for the candlesticks out of tissue paper and how you made baskets in the shape of hearts out of shiny paper for hanging on the Christmas tree and a crib with grass seed sown on blotting paper—"But we always forget to sow the grass early enough, and last year we had to put moss around the stable instead, and the baby Jesus was lost, so we had to use a little plastic doll of mine, but it had white socks and black shoes on and it looked so silly lying there in the crib that we had to cover it up with a little blanket of moss!

"And we bake lots of cookies and cakes before Christmas," Sara continued, "and I help Mother brush them with white of egg and sprinkle them with sugar and almonds . . . and I can make ginger biscuits all by myself, and there is a smell of ginger biscuits in the whole house, and Dad also helps—he makes the big hearts and writes our names on them with white icing-sugar. And there is a smell of sealing wax and hyacinths and Christmas tree, and our yellow sofa is almost full of presents." Sara fell silent, quite overcome by her own description.

151

"When my father was alive—it . . . it was long ago—he took us to our uncle in Isfahan . . . a big city . . . to celebrate the New Year," Gunilla suddenly said very softly.

"Oh," Sara replied, her heart beating faster. Christmas was completely forgotten. "Yes?"

"Yes, you see," Gunilla continued with some hesitation. "Mohammedans don't celebrate Christmas, but New Year—No Ruz—but the New Year is not at the same time as yours in January. It is really . . . it is a spring festival. Our New Year begins on the twenty-first of March."

"How very strange!"

"And everybody is very happy, and they have fireworks and . . . whatever it's called when you have big fires in the streets and the squares . . ."

"Bonfires you mean."

"We had those in our village, too, of course, but in Isfahan everything was much bigger and better. People say that they are burning all the unpleasant things that have happened during the year. And then we have an outing to the country with food in a basket, and it's great fun . . . and before that everybody gives each other cards and flowers and goldfish . . .

"My uncle gave me a bowl—a beautiful bowl with a shining green base and two goldfish. My uncle was rich . . . he wore a long blue robe and a yellow turban.

"He walked around with us in the town and showed us all the beautiful houses and churches and minarets,

152

and most beautiful of all was the mosque of the Shah with a bright blue cupola—it was by a huge square with arcades all around it.

"I don't remember very well because I was young, but what I remember most are those long straight arrows of light, the rockets, that shot off little red and blue balls into the sky and tiny little suns that went around and around.

"People shouted and pushed, and I dropped my goldfish bowl, and all the water ran out and the fishes lay there on the ground flapping with their tails, but my Uncle got some more water from the big fountain with flowers around it, and then he bought silver bracelets for Mother and Granny in the bazaars, you know . . . lovely silver, like lace, with tiny blue stones and green ones . . . and they were very pretty."

Gunilla's words came more and more slowly until she finally stopped talking altogether.

Perhaps she was asleep. Sara didn't dare to say a word.

She lay there wide awake, listening to the summer storm, feeling completely happy.